DOOM STAR
Number Two

Richard S. Meyers

CARLYLE • NEW YORK

This is a work of fiction. All the characters and events portrayed in this book are fictional, and any resemblance to real people or incidents is purely coincidental.

Copyright © 1979 by Richard S. Meyers

CARLYLE BOOKS are published by
Siena Publishing Corp.
New York, New York

ISBN: 0-503-07050-5

Printed in The United States of America

Cover design: Roy Kuhlman

DOOM STAR
Number Two

CHAPTER ONE

The man with one nostril took one look at the five-foot cat sitting at the table, gasped, "the Last in Line," and fainted dead away.

When the cat, a female feline from the nearly mythical planet of Mandarin, managed to revive him, he took his second look, uttered the same four words, "the Last in Line," then his eyes rolled up into their sockets.

"No, friend," said the feline in her easy, alto tones, "the name is Napoleon. Just Napoleon. Are you all right?"

"The Last in Line, the Last in Line," the man mumbled, shivering as if deathly chilled, "the Last in Line."

The feline threw a glance at her companion, a stocky, man with lines like canals across his face his black beard and muscles like coiled bunches of hemp. She shrugged. He placed his solid hands under the quivering man's shoulders and lifted him up into a chair. Napoleon glanced around to see if the incident had any effect on the other patrons of the eating establishment. Every eye and sensor was glued on her.

She waved, pointed at herself, and said, "the Last in Line." Meanwhile the man had regained his composure enough to sit up like a rod had been bashed across his spinal column and grab her arm like his hands had been magnetized.

Before the man could speak, the feline's companion made a short punch to the poor fellow's elbows, smashing the hands off the furry arms and nearly throwing the man out of the chair.

"Harlan," reprimanded the cat, "please. That wasn't necessary."

"Sorry," he apologized, his muscular figure actually sloped over in supplication. "Force of habit, I guess."

"Harlan," Napoleon repeated. "We've been in space the last two years. We haven't had a battle of any sort in almost twice that."

"Old habits die hard," the black-bearded man mumbled.

During the conversation, the man in the chair had regained his breath. His hands sought the feline's arm again, but just for a moment. With one look from the bearded man, he forcefully dropped them to the table.

"Do not make light of the Last in Line," he intoned. "You, out of all, should not treat his dying lightly."

Napoleon, her green eyes flashing and her

golden, striped tail lashing, turned on the quaking intoner.

"The Last in Line?" she queried. "Who's dying? What are you talking about?"

"Go to him," pleaded the man, as if she hadn't spoken. "I implore you, he needs you." His hands rose to her face, the fingers vibrating like rung bells. Her visage, however, held only confused ignorance. "I know what's troubling you!" the man suddenly exclaimed, his hands clapping together. "I will prepare your way! Do not worry, I will tell him of your coming!"

Then, before Napoleon could utter another word or the bearded man could grab him, the one nostriled figure was up and out the door.

The two discussed the incident later, on the way back to their ship. The Tiger's Eye, the new spacecraft built especially for Napoleon, was in land docking, taking on supplies and making needed updates in the equipment. Thanks to the funny laws of faster-than-light space travel, for every one year one spends in space, ten years pass on any fixed point, most notably on orbiting planets. So the world one may have left for a few months in hyper-space is not the world one will probably return to.

"Harlan," Napoleon said, squeezing the atmosphere bottle under her nose, "I felt this planet would probably be fairly strange, but I've never seen people like this before. Then again, what should I expect from a world named Finally?"

"It's part of the legend," Harlan Trigor

replied, partaking of his own squeeze-bottle of supplemental air. "When man was first sent out into the stars, way before the Earth's Great Natural Disaster, ships without the O'Neil faster-than-light drive would drift for generations before finding a habitable planet. Hence names like Finally."

And hence things like the atmosphere bottles. As a very bored spaceport official explained to them on their arrival, although the remnants of humanity had evolved eons before to accept the less-than-perfect air ratios on Finally, visitors would often feel faint or sick without some vital ingredients pressed within the squeeze bottles. They came free of charge to every tourist who paid the docking price.

"You think that guy was an off-worlder?" the feline asked.

"I'm not sure," said Harlan. "He had the one nostril in the middle of the big nose like everybody else here, but he seemed to have a different tinge than the others. Did you notice?"

"Yes. He was on the blue side. And he talked very softly, did *you* notice that?"

"I'm sorry," whispered Harlan. "I couldn't hear you. What's that you say?"

Napoleon had no time to retort, for they had come back to their landed ship, the Tiger's Eye. It was in the same shape and the same color as the gem: oblong gold with a bronze streak around the middle which marked the entrance. It was a large spaceship, held up on either end by crisscrossing scaffolding, erected by the eager spaceport officials. They didn't get many visitors on the main planet of Finally, so Napoleon's ship was given extra special care and allowed to rest almost in the center of the main city.

The one-nostriled cleaners deferred to the sleek, fur-covered creature in the rust-colored leotard with the green and brown patch on the left breast. Harlan marched right behind her, a two-nostriled model of manhood, trained to be one of his solar system's best warriors. Together, they made quite a sinewy, attractive pair.

Harlan's training and Napoleon's patch both eminated from the same planet, a lush garden world on the edge of the known galaxy known as Destiny. Even here, among the uncharted regions of space to which Destiny served as a gateway, its legend and fame was sung and proclaimed. On almost every man-harboring world, Destiny and its denizens were recognized. Of course, a five-foot tall intelligent cat accompanied by a man who could tear your face off without your knowing it, is a pretty hard combination to ignore.

Napoleon and Harlan moved into the ship's control room together, admiring the gleaming new fittings in the U-shaped bridge. The entire rear of the area was taken up by a curling wall of bright machinery, highlighted by a bright red slot in the middle. It was from this area that a new voice sounded.

"Took you long enough."

Napoleon and Harlan continued to look over

the added material and neither turned.

"Pardon?" said Harlan.

"Mess. . ." Napoleon intoned warningly.

"It's not easy to watch over all these people, you know," Mess, the on-board computer, continued. "Where were you all this time? I was just about out of my console with worry."

"We told you," said Harlan, still not deeming the machine worthy of a direct look, "we went out to find something to eat. And you need not have worried. Your mistress was quite safe with me."

A squeal was emitted from a speaker just above Harlan's head, sounding like a cross between sheet metal being ripped in half and the slaughtering of a spaceport official. It was one of Mess's myriad ways to express itself. "Well," it continued, hurt seeming to color every word, "why couldn't you have asked me? I could have made up something."

"Mess," answered Napoleon, finally turning to face the computer's console. "We've been asking you for the last two years. We wanted something a little less familiar."

"You never like my experiments," Mess retorted. "You never seemed to want diversity before. All you ever wanted was the same old thing. So I gave it to you. Is that a crime?"

Napoleon threw up her paws in defeat and continued to test the new additions while Mess fell into an electrical sulk. M.E.S.S., originally titled the Multi-unit Electrical System for Space travel, then called the Many Excuses to Save itSelf when it was discovered to be paranoid, had recently entered its maternal phase after an accident back on Destiny. Now, instead of wanting to destroy anything that got near it, Mess wanted to destroy anything that got near Napoleon.

The feline in question sank into her pilot's chair, the one with the indented hole in the back for her tail, and started practical tests. Harlan moved back toward the rear of the room where nine feet of what looked like statue-shaped space rock stood. The large slate-colored hunk was shaped vaguely like a man except that neither arms nor legs were visible. And where the head should have been was a hole and a cup-shaped piece of rock, hanging down from the neck area, like a thrown-back parka hood.

As Napoleon double checked the warning systems, food stores, escape 'eyes,' and related circuitry, Harlan nimbly leaped up the monolith-like slab and started climbing down inside it. Soon he was shoulder deep in the piece of space debris and was pulling a netting of gray tubes across his head. As the gridded mask settled on his face, the gray turned blue and green and started pulsating like living veins. Then the entire rock seemed to come alive.

Harlan was back in his natural habitat, as Napoleon was in hers. She was a feline space traveler, searching for a purpose in her life. He was Destiny's greatest "space bullet," a soldier whose one purpose was to protect the beautiful things in life. The beautiful things on his home world had been the planet itself: a fable

11

for trouble-weary astronauts, a target for power-hungry space pirates, and a home for a race of Earth-descended human beings. A select few evolved into the double-jointed, muscular species that enabled them to protect the planet by fighting in the upper atmosphere, completely at one with their self-contained rocket ship and armament known as a space bullet. Inside the suit, Harlan was at all-powerful, all-knowing peace.

While lovingly checking over his own, personal ship, Harlan began to sing a bit from his corps anthem, "The Legend of the Space Bullets".

From the womb we are born,
It is what we must be;
We're divers for glory,
And the sky is our sea.

"There he goes again," Mess complained.

Napoleon hastily contributed a means to keep the computer occupied. "Is the ship space-worthy?" she asked.

"Of course," replied Mess, with a slight undertone of injury.

"Can we take off any time?"

"Isn't that the same thing you just asked me?"

Napoleon knew that her consideration had lead her into one of the computer's guilt traps. Now she'd have to explain the difference. "Mess," she began sweetly. "Space-worthy referred to all the new equipment and check-ups we performed on this dismal planet. Taking off involves a lot more than that."

12

"Such as?"

"Such as clearances and making sure we don't crush any unsuspecting workmen who might still be around!" the feline flared.

"According to my information," returned Mess icily, "based on prior circumstances and materials imprinted on my circuits by Dr. Palsy-Drake at the date of my conception and Larry Baker at the date of my resurrection, to be space-worthy is to be capable of taking off and to be capable of taking off means that all relative complications have been met."

"You mean we're all ready to go?" Napoleon pressed, as Harlan began to climb out of his suit.

"I'm hurt that you should think otherwise," replied the computer's haughty voice.

"You don't have feelings," cut in Harlan flatly as he began to secure the suit with clamps against the opposite wall.

"Yes, I do!" it cried. "Yes, I do! I proved it on Destiny!" The computer had overcome its programmed rule of self-preservation before all to save its caretakers. As a result, it had been blasted apart, then later put back together by Larry Baker with some telling differences.

"A calculated gamble on your part," Harlan explained. "You knew you'd never make it out of that wilderness. Your only hope was to return and try to help."

There was a long, cold, silent pause from the computer console, during which Napoleon shot Harlan laser-sharp looks while Harlan looked innocently at the ceiling and continued to tend his suit. Finally the machine spoke up.

"How . . . *dare* . . . you!" it spat electronically, with barely controlled rage. "After all I have done for you, to be so callous, so thoughtless. . . ." The machine's voice trailed off, but with just a pause to change the pace of its words. "That's it!" it then said briskly. "It's over. I can see I'm not appreciated around here. Why don't you just disconnect me? Go ahead, I'm ready. Disconnect me. Now, right now. Drive the wrench in. Go ahead."

"Would you two just stop it?" Napoleon howled. "Harlan, quit baiting it. And Mess, please! You're not my mother. You're not anybody's mother. Let's damper down a little bit on the guilt program, all right?"

She silently cursed Larry Baker for caring so much about her. Memories of his long, peaceful face began to assail her. They had been a team on Earth. An Earth millions of light-years away now, but then it had been important, vital, and dangerous. She was the only feline alive in the galaxy. Her sisters had been wiped out by genetic experiments and she was sought and lusted after by every vice-lord and government official imaginable. This was long after the Great Natural Disaster, so females, *any* females were premium.

He was an artificial. One of the best of that kind, but artificial nevertheless; a made commodity, one of the things Earth AND (After Natural Disaster) specialized in. Subsequent to all the wars, all the destruction, all the earthquakes, and everything else Mother

14

Nature and humanity's own stupidity could throw at the tiny world, the remaining military and government people (the only people with time enough to avoid the inevitable) started exporting the spawn of their laboratories.

Larry and she had escaped that prison, escaped the hell of the doom star, Sol, in a ship called the Black Hole, only to fight to save another solar system. After all the fighting, Larry was the only one to find happiness. He remained on Destiny, partner to Harlan's beautiful sister, and became the ruling father of a new world. It was hard for the feline to comprehend that he might be two decades older now—maybe even dead—while she had only been gone two years.

But he had left a little of himself behind in Mess. Restructuring it for her ship, he had programmed a maternal instinct into the machine. He had not counted on that motherly attitude combining with the computer's natural paranoia. And that team was enough to drive anything crazy. It made for a lively two years.

"Things are ready, then," the feline continued. "All right, then, let's go!"

"Where to?" Harlan innocently inquired, moving over to his copilot's position.

"Anywhere," Napoleon replied, stabbing a tenser square on her console. Larry, when building the Tiger's Eye's new control board, replaced all the buttons, dials and switches with heat-sensitive squares, squares that responded to only pre-programmed touches. In

15

this case, the only two who could fly the Tiger's Eye were the feline and the space bullet. "Finally Central City Spaceport," Napoleon called. "We're leaving."

She waited a few minutes for the double clicks that signified "message received." Instead there was a longer pause than usual and a voice speaking in a English said, "Tiger's Eye, you are cleared to travel to the second moon."

Napoleon had already started instigating takeoff procedures and had to forcibly stop herself from shooting right off the planet. "What?" she spat, the very model of feminine verbosity.

"Cleared to shuttle to Finally Finished, the second moon."

"What's the first moon called?" Harlan mumbled.

"Finally Over," Mess answered.

Napoleon jabbed the communications tensor again. "Finally Central," she growled, "what's this about? I made no arrangements to jaunt to any moon."

"Tiger's Eye," returned the voice on the communications line, "we have duly received your shuttle request, acknowledged it and now have a space lane open for you."

Napoleon cut the connection and spun to face Mess's console, her furry visage crunched into suspicion.

"What are you looking at?" the computer inquired. "I certainly had nothing to do with this."

Harlan put a hand on the feline's arm. She

turned to see her communication tensor flashing. She pushed it.

"Tiger's Eye, this is Finally Spaceport," said a new voice. "Please shuttle to the second moon or give up your place in the lane. We have plenty of others wanting to make the flight."

"What's the attraction?" Harlan asked under his breath, but the sensitive machinery picked it up.

"Tiger's Eye, you have put in for a travel lane to Finally Finished," said the spaceport representative by way of reply, "paying a very high fee, I might add, for almost immediate privilege. We were more than happy to schedule you, but now, for some reason, you are holding up all the transportation."

Napoleon looked to Harlan in confusion, then started tapping the tensor. "Just wait awhile, Finally Central. There seems to be some difficulty here." She switched out the communication link.

"This fellow is talking like there's no reason possible for not wanting to visit their second moon," said Harlan.

"And for such a lifeless world, Finally Finished seems to be overpopulated with guests," Napoleon added. "Interesting. Mess, you sure you had nothing to do with this?"

The computer squealed indignantly.

"The Last in Line," said Harlan.

"What?" asked Napoleon.

"The Last in Line, you remember. The little blue man. He said he was going to prepare your way."

"That's right. He was going to tell him that I was coming. That's who put up the 'high fee' and arranged the 'immediate scheduling.' Why, that little booger."

The tensor had nearly strobed out by the time Napoleon had tapped it again. Before the spaceport officials could bluster, Napoleon said in her smoothest tones, "Sorry for the confusion, Finally Central. The problem has been allieviated and we are departing now." Then, without a thank you, she cut the lines and threw the takeoff complexities to Mess.

She had stared at her control board for thirty seconds before Harlan interrupted her smirking reverie.

"Napoleon, what are you planning? I know that evil, insulted look on your face."

The gold-green cat eyes turned toward the copilot, her lightly furred brows arching down in righteous anger. "Nothing controls my life, Harlan."

"Napoleon," the soldier sighed, his broad shoulders hunching forward, "please. I've told you before and I'll tell you again. Everything is not a plot to control you. Sometimes things happen because of a consideration, a practicality, or, probably in this case, a mistake."

"Nothing controls my life," the feline calmly repeated.

The space bullet sighed again, then leaned back in his chair. "What are you going to do?"

"I'll visit the second moon, all right. I'll even find out about this last in line thing, but I'll do it on my terms, my way."

18

"Are you two finished conferring?" whined Mess. "I'd like to take off now."

As the nine-foot-tall piece of space debris and the five-foot-tall cat walked side by side, the ground rolled. The first hunk of dirt coiled itself into a ball and flew at the two figures. Harlan, completely enshrined in his space bullet, simply rose above the fistlike mixture of stone and soil, but Napoleon wasn't so lucky. Weighed down by a beamer strapped across her back and a spitter in a holster around her waist, she barely had the time or the strength to leap straight up in the air.

Howling madly in a fit of anger and surprise, she rose almost seven feet and rolled, but the swinging ball of dirt managed to connect with her shoulder and sent her spinning back five feet. The next second a green bolt struck out from the floating piece of space debris, smashing and spreading the coiled mass of ground into a clear ball of dirt and dust. A second after that, a crackling explosion was heard across the plain. And a second after that Harlan's quiet voice spoke from the empty air.

"*Now* will you let me carry you?"

Napoleon sat on her haunches, rubbing her left shoulder with one fur-covered paw. Her strawberry blond fur looked luminous on the moon, Finally's second satellite, because of the rich atmosphere and its closer proximity to the sun. "No," she growled stubbornly, "I said I'd walk and I'm going to."

19

Her voice was an animal-like screech because of the lancing pain the dirt fist and subsequent fall had caused, befitting the regally sensual, fur- and whiskered-covered face from which it had eminated. She glanced down to see if there were any outward signs of wounds. Finding none, she pulled her boot-covered legs out from under her coiled tail, straightened her rust-colored leotard from under her weapons, then rose.

"Leave Mess in the ship," she mimicked sarcastically toward the floating space bullet, looking, to anything else, like a unfinished statue of a man, hovering a foot and a half off the moon's surface. "I can detect oncoming threats. I can carry you for protection. Well, what happened, Harlaneeeeeeowwww!"

As she was finishing her question, another mound of earth swung at her. She was just able to jump high enough to skid across the top, then rolled down the other side as her weapons bounced atop her. The space bullet waited until she had come to a standstill, then repeated its destructive process. Another bolt, another thunderclap, and another descending cloud of brown litter.

The cat instantly found her feet and scrambled over to where Harlan floated, scratching dirt out of her face. By the time she was able to speak, it was in the form of several stout curses.

"By the Earth Father! By the Destiny Mother! *By Cheshire!* What is going on? What is this, an earthquake?" The space bullet hovered silently for a moment, then shook once.

"No visual or sensory signs of that, Napoleon," came Harlan's voice from the general direction of the top of the bullet. "If the ground hadn't moved, I would not have had any evidence of it in here." The top foot and a half of the suit began to turn to the left.

The feline slapped the suit on the side. "Well, then, check yourself! This could be dangerous."

The top of the space debris rose, then fell back, like a parka hood thrown off, revealing Harlan's bearded head. "I have checked," he called down, "and double checked. No thinking matter in this ground of any kind. Whatever's happening, it isn't the work of a hidden brain. But for safety's sake, I'd better carry you and fly us the rest of the way."

"No, I can make it, we just need to know what this stuff is."

"Napoleon, I see no reason for you to be so independent. Especially since it's so useless right now."

"I repeat, I'll wallllllowwwwk!"

Two mounds of dirt had suddenly risen to a height of six feet and come at the feline from either direction. She leaped backwards, flipped over and landed on all fours, her weapons pounding her sides and her tail straight up. The two mounds smacked into each other like ocean waves and diminished back into the ground.

"Harlan," she howled, "let's try to give me a

little warning on those, will you?"

"Something odd is going on," Harlan said more to himself than his companion, his eyes cast down into his suit. His head covering suddenly rose again and screwed itself back on. "Keep an eye out for a moment. will you, Napoleon?"

The feline pulled her beamer rifle down and opened the ring at the butt of the barrel to the widest aperture. She then held the weapon loosely at her side and turned in a semicircle, her eyelids lowering. She turned back to look up at the space bullet and saw a huge mound of ground rear up behind the floating figure and let the hunk of stone have it square in the back.

She managed to howl once before jumping back, pulling her beamer up and firing. The debris-suited space bullet disappeared in a whirlpool of dark, dirty wind as the orange beam of her weapon sliced off a large hunk of dirt. The rest of the pile exploded out around the space bullet, then fell forward, on a collision course with the cat.

Her left paw shot out and spun the barrel wheel, while her right paw contracted spastically, cutting a small, orange-tinged hole in the midst of the huge, falling ball. Pulling the beamer to her chest, she leaped through the opening she had made with the grace of a lead-weighted ballerina.

The mound of dirt crashed to the ground, bursting like a mud ball with little drops flying off it like brown mercury. It undulated across the surface of the moon, like a hand caressing its lover's body, then swirled back into it, as if it had never existed.

Napoleon rolled to her feet, and silently cursed the weapons weighing her down, turned to make sure no other mounds were conspiring against her, then returned to the hovering space bullet's side.

"Trouble," said Harlan.

"You're telling me?"

"No, I mean more than that. I can't tell where they're coming from or when they're going to attack. Their forms simply don't register inside the suit."

Before the stunned feline had time to react, she felt herself spinning off the ground. She twisted in mid-air to see a hurtling pile of dirt swinging below her and the entire landscape diminishing in size. She was flying outwards in the grip of the space bullet.

As was common with the suit's abilities, she hadn't even seen the rocklike monolith sprout arms. Further, she did not know how they were able to move with the grace of flesh and no matter how hard Harlan had tried, he couldn't explain coherently. All either of them knew for sure was the suit's incredible power and Harlan's ability to harness it from within, using every muscle across his body.

Napoleon wrapped her limbs across his torso, her tail lashing in the air and said, "Thank you very much, Harlan. You can put me down now."

"No, thank *you* very much," he replied. "I

really think it would be best for all concerned to get back to the ship until we know what we're up against here. You don't seem to understand. I can't *see* these things!"

As he spoke, the sun disappeared. Total shadow fell across the flying pair and Napoleon twisted in the space bullet's grip to see why.

"Uh-oh," she said.

"What's the matter?"

"Harlan, take off your top, quickly. And pick up speed. Now!"

Hearing the urgency in her voice, the space bullet went faster and unscrewed his top. As his head appeared he saw it. Replacing the sun and the sky was a hurtling, ever-growing slab of churning dirt, pulling itself into a vengeful tidal wave of a mountain. And it was coming right at them.

"Why didn't anything *tell* us about this!" Napoleon howled, her now-unsheathed claws ineffectually digging into the space bullet, her legs scrambling. The huge, moving mountain had gained momentum and height even in the short amount of time it took her to speak. Harlan didn't bother to answer, he just screwed himself back into the suit and picked up speed.

"I can't find the ship properly without total concentration," he explained. "You hold on tight and keep me informed. I'll signal ahead to Mess and get us space-ready." Two more arms seperated themselves from the space bullet's torsolike liquid marble and held Napoleon's shoulders, back, pelvis, and legs in

24

a closed-off grid. He arched his body down and shot off.

The speed of his flight nearly tore the feline out of his grasp, but the sight of the animated inanimate mountain chasing them did wonders for her grip. "Faster," she managed to blurt, "faster."

"I can't go any faster," he cried. "I'll lose you. You'd be suffocated by the speed." The moving mountain had begun to cast its shadow across the space bullet's broad back.

"You have to," Napoleon screeched, not able to hear her own voice in the howl of the wind. "It's catching up!"

She turned her head and screwed open her eyes to look beyond his protective form. The huge mound of dirt was coursing just behind them, looking like a gigantic digestive track. Unrecognizable things would turn in and out of its whirring insides, spinning rocks and foilage all around them. Napoleon looked down, but Harlan had reached such an altitude that the planet below had become a patchwork quilt of geometric shapes. She twisted back to the space bullet's chest.

"Blast it!" she called. "It's directly in back of me. Give it everything you've got!"

"It's ... too ... close," she heard his crackling reply.

"Then slice it up," she pleaded. "Disintegrate it!" She had seen his destructive power on Earth, on Destiny and elsewhere; she couldn't understand why he wasn't implementing his strength now.

25

She knew he was speaking some more but in the roar of their flight the words were unintelligible and the titanic threat was looming.

"Move me," she gasped. "Move me over."

The artificial limbs slid the feline over to the space bullet's right side.

"Hand me my beamer," she instructed.

The hands complied. The wind pressure against her body turned the horizon and the ground below into a red-tinged haze, but all she was intent on now was the approaching mammoth mound and the barrel of her weapon.

"Faster," she painfully whispered, arching her body around until she faced the black and brown hulk behind her. "Faster." She spun the beam widener to its greatest aperture, than pushed the weapon out in front of her with both paws. Wide swaths of orange light began slicing out.

They seemed to slide into the brown moving mass, having almost no visual effect. Any dirt she displaced was immediately replaced by more. The range was too far to create any sizable hole and the mountain kept changing, spinning in on itself like a rock tornado. She looked up, but she couldn't see the top of the movable mountain. In hopeless anger, she pointed her beamer at the sky and started pulling the beam across the width of the pursuing mound like a scyth.

"The sides!" she heard Harlan's distant voice call. "Start . . . cutting . . . awa . . . a . . . sides. . . ."

Her arm felt like feather-light iron—heavy and immovable but still, somehow, separate from her body. Her trigger claw seemed to have a life of its own, since the brain commanding it had long fogged over. One thought filtered down to the feline consciousness. What had happened to the space bullet's power? Why wasn't it doing anything but flying?

The beamer had begun to cut away at the sides of the mountain, Napoleon's sharp, arching strokes pulling huge hunks of dirt off the main body until the tall structure was getting very thin in the middle. Even so, it seemed to be getting larger at every moment.

Suddenly Napoleon realized it *was* getting larger at every moment. The pressure against her body was lightening as well. She could breath, see and think again, but it wasn't because of strength or willpower. The space bullet was slowing down. The feline quickly twisted around and glared over his shoulders, expecting the Tiger's Eye to be looming large. The ship was nowhere in sight.

"What are you doing?" she screamed at the blank, slate-colored face. "Harlan, what's the matter?"

There was no reply.

When she looked back at the mountainous mound of ground, it had leaned over the space bullet's hurtling form, still moving forward itself. Even as she watched, the weakened center section of the structure, eaten away by her beamer, began to crumble and fall toward them.

"Harlan!" she cried at the top of her lungs. "Roll! Barrel roll out of the way! Now!"

There was no response.

She desperately twisted in his grasp and saw that the ground was beginning to rise up toward them. The space bullet was no longer flying; it was falling. She snapped her head back toward the breaking, crashing mountain. Almost all light had been snuffed out by its descent. They were trapped. Napoleon suddenly felt certain that Harlan had died.

Every hair on her fur-covered body stood straight up. Her pupils became gemlike slits. She dropped her beamer and started pounding on his chest area, mewing pitiously.

"Harlan, Harlan, Harlan, Harlan, Harlan, Harlan. . . ."

Suddenly his body started spinning, turned by the funnel of air between the rapidly approaching surface of the planet and the falling slab of earth.

Then the ground and the moving mountain met.

CHAPTER TWO

The feline was half right.

The space bullet had died, but Harlan Trigor still lived. He had felt the unexplainable loss of power in the suit as soon as he had lifted Napoleon off the moon's surface. He had noticed a slight degeneration of his powers for some time, but had decided the loss of ability was due to his own space fatigue. But as he flew from the unseen, unsensed mountain, he began to realize the truth. His shell was dying.

Inside the suit, inside the darkness that rivaled death, Harlan felt the blackness of purgatory touch him. And, for the first time since becoming a space bullet so long ago, he felt fear. A fear that clung to his brain, deadening his responses and dulling his reflexes. He felt himself being buried alive in a coffin of armor.

A tiny flicker lit up in the corner of one eye.

Then another off to his right. Then another below him. Still another off in the recess of his suit as, bit by bit, the life force that ran the space bullet winked out. There was just a little bit of power left. Harlan's every muscle strained to pull that power up, to send it to the head mechanism and free himself.

He had not felt the moving mountain smash him to the ground. He had not felt the feline's desperate fists pounding across his torso. He had not felt the enormous weight of the dirt push him deep into the soil. He had not felt the soil give way until the suit crashed through the ceiling of an underground cave. He had not felt the concussion as the suit crashed into a bed of blue crystal. He had felt nothing since his suit gave out.

He had not seen the huge cavern of blue crystals, stalactites and stalagmites shatter into millions of singing gems on his explosive arrival. He had not heard the frightful roar of his entrance shatter walls of blue stone into spinning shards. He had not heard the scream of the explosion echo down through the caverns, deafening the faithful. He was completely cut off, buried in his space bullet.

Harlan had nurtured the flicker of power into a small flame with the strength of his ability. The head of the suit began to turn. Slowly but steadily the top section spun until a sliver of blue, luminous light shone across his cheek. Finally the head fell off and he heard a gasp. It was his own. His suit lay against one broken wall of solid blue, transparent stone, reflecting back the image of hundreds of one-nostriled men, women and children lining the rest of the cavern.

Harlan hauled imself out of the space bullet unsteadily. As he pulled, the watching throng moved back, horror coloring their blue faces. By the time he reached his feet, the crowd looked as if a riot would follow immediately, but otherwise they uttered no sound. Harlan looked down to his suit. It had turned from its vibrant slate color to a slick, oily gray— the color of ash.

It lay on its side, a dead carcass, but there, still in its four arms, was Napoleon—unconscious and bleeding from the nose and mouth. Harlan spun wildly toward the onlooking crowd, his arms raised and pleading.

"Please," he said, but his voice was taken by the slick walls and empty halls and echoed dozens of times over, making even that one word totally incomprehensible. The violence of the sudden, sharp echo, magnified many times and hardly diminishing as it flew from cave to cave, poked annoyingly at the man's eardrums.

Confused and in shock, Harlan stumbled back and fell across the cave wall, one blue crystal stalagmite scraping his side. Suddenly, possessed of unexpected strength, Harlan grabbed the stalagmite, hurled it above his head like a club, then brought it down on the arms of his suit with a shattering force.

The crowds' hands flew up to their ears as the space bullet's four arms, the stalagmite and the silence exploded with an ear shattering roar. Harlan was picked up and hurled back against the wall as the crowd fell to its knees. Napoleon, still unconscious and now also bleeding from the ears, dropped to the blue bed of crystals. She landed on her back, streaks of red coursing across her golden face.

As the sound was sucked into the deepest recess of the cavern, a barely conscious Harlan saw the crowd rise again and look upon the face of the feline. As they approached her small, wounded figure, another sound rose up— one far greater and more terrible than anything that had preceeded. The entire crowd fell to its knees and started to pay supplicatory honor to the barely living Napoleon.

She was locked in a cage. She felt herself falling in a bottomless tunnel, the horror being that there was no light at the end. She spun down, the walls coming closer and closer until her head and feet began to scrape along the side. But she didn't slow down and she wasn't even wounded. The tunnel kept getting smaller and more and more of her began to scrape off, but she felt no pain. Finally she saw herself falling inside the walls of the tunnel, with pieces of her body spreading out in all directions. Then she woke up.

Napoleon was lying on a huge mat with her hands at her sides and her legs slightly spread. Her wrists, ankles and legs, just above the knees, were strapped down. And there was a plush pad across her mouth, attached to the back of her neck. Immediately her claws came out and she began tearing her limbs back and forth. From her right side came a whisper of noise and then a head was leaning by her ear.

"Please, do not struggle," said a barely audible voice. "It is for your own good."

The feline turned—at least that part of her was not restrained—and looked into the biggest blue eyes she had ever seen on a human. They looked like two gems stuck in the middle of two spotlights. The rest of the face was attractive but, thankfully, not as striking. The girl's visage was haloed by brown hair down to her shoulders, and her wide, thin lips smiled.

"You are in the Temple of Quiet Ice," she told Napoleon, again with an incredibly soft voice, "where every sound can be torture. The restraints are necessary so you do not thrash or cry out in your sleep, wounding your already delicate senses. You are lucky to be alive."

Napoleon wanted to reply, but the soft gag prevented it, so she looked around instead. All about the large, oblong room were decorations of blue stones. Even the mat she lay upon was given a hollowed-out foundation of blue rock. Other than the makeshift bed and one large blue boulder which served as a table, the cave-like room was devoid of furnishing.

"I will unfix you now," whispered the brunette. "If you wish to converse, please lean close to my ear and speak as quietly as possible. Even better, use sign lanquage."

33

The girl touched each of Napoleon's bounds with a small piece of blue stone she secreted from her tunic and the straps just fell away. Reading the feline's perplexed face, the girl began working on her muzzle, explaining, "Our quiet ice has some amazing properties. In some cases, stones of any size can be magnetized to unbreakable strength, but the touch of this lodestone can neutralize it."

By the end of her lecture, Napoleon was completely free, and, sitting up, she discovered she was totally naked. But, as usual, her fur kept her warm and others demure. She rose to her knees and leaned over the girl's ear. "Who are you?" she asked. The girl leaned back to the feline's ear.

"I go by no name, since we do not call to each other here. At the moment, I have been honored to tend to your needs and see to your recovery. Your arrival to our temple was not an easy one."

Napoleon rose to her feet to try out her rested body, but even as she moved, the nameless brunette kept pace with her and kept speaking in her ear.

"We saw the demon body fall off the new man," she explained. "And the new man free you from the demon's clutches. He suffered in the process but is recovering now too. We recognized you right away and naturally took steps to insure your comfort. Proper attire has already been prepared and a meeting with the Last in Line has already been arranged. If you are hungry, we have prepared sustenance for

34

you and I shall be your guide anywhere you wish to go in our temple."

Napoleon stopped flexing and faced the brunette. It was like listening to your own long-winded conscience, but the feline figured that in a cavern where sound was dangerous, one might attempt to answer every question at once, so no more dialogue would be necessary. Her stomach growled, making a slight echo which lasted far longer than any echo she had ever created on Earth. So Napoleon rubbed her stomach in what she hoped was a universal sign of hunger and moved her arm forward, silently asking for the brunette to lead the way.

Harlan was seated at the blue-stone table after Napoleon had been led through more than a dozen caverns. He put his finger up to his lips, smiled and then waved. Not standing on ceremony, she leaped right up to him, pulled him to his feet and hugged him for all she was worth.

"Are you all right?" she asked, then lived to regret it.

The words echoed over and over in the confined space until she had to drop her arms and cover her ears. The sound then seemed to move physically out of the room and traveled in all directions. The brunette with no name moved in.

"Soon every member of the Temple will hear your words with the magnified volume they picked up here. Thankfully they will hear it coming and protect themselves accordingly. *Please* whisper."

Napoleon gave her an A-O.K. sign with her claws, then sat down next to Harlan, smiling wanly. She leaned close to his ear. "What happened?"

"My suit died."

The feline reared back to look into her companion's face. He shrugged and leaned over to her ear.

"I've been able to get over it while you recovered. I ... uh ... felt worse about you than I did about me. That helped."

Still, Napoleon could imagine what it must have been like to lose his space-bullet armor. It would be like losing your mother, your natural defenses, and your best friend all on the same day. You felt yourself the prime target for the first germ that passed by. The feline leaned back and rubbed against his side.

"No, really, really, it's all right," he whispered. "Eat."

They looked into each other's eyes. The care they both found there made them want to speak further, but the environment was prohibitive. They ate. Most of the meal was vegetable in nature with a touch of fruit here and there, but it was all revitalizing. By the end of the meal, Napoleon's tail was lashing with energy.

"So what happens now?" she whispered to the brunette, who was beginning to look left out.

"We wait."

"For what?"

"For his commandment."

36

For a girl who had been so helpful before, her new responses were strangely hesitant, the feline thought.

"For whose commandment?" she pressed.

"The . . . Last in Line."

Napoleon looked at the brunette and mouthed a silent, "Oh," then turned to Harlan and furrowed her brow in perplexity. He signaled her to lean in.

"It's their religion," he explained quietly. "This is their temple. The only difference between their religion and our religion is that our God is imagined and theirs is dying in a room somewhere. To speak his name lightly or at all is pretty serious stuff for them."

"That's the Last in Line? Their God?"

"It seems so. He supposedly has all sorts of great power, like the ability to move mountains. You get it?"

Napoleon raised her eyebrows so Harlan could see, then moved back to his ear. Their conversation looked like a new dance or the fastest necking on record.

"Where do I fit in?"

"Now there you've got me, but they've been treating you very well. This is the first time I've seen you since the . . . accident."

"Well, if I'm so special, why did their hot deity sic his mountains on us?"

The conversation was suddenly interrupted by a sweeping wind which seemed to pull the brunette right out of her chair. She frantically shushed the two and moved to the rocky entrance of the cave. She turned once to smile

37

benignly at Napoleon, then turned to face the approaching wind.

The feline heard a distant voice. It was deep, throaty, and graveled by the passing of time. As the echo moved from cavern to cavern, she heard that it was a commanding voice, a voice, even at this low volume, which could be respected and followed. Somewhere, deep inside her, she felt a recognition at the sound.

Finally the word reached the room. It was only one word, but, not surprisingly after such a long journey, it spoke volumes.

"Come," said the voice.

Napoleon was led by the brunette to a gigantic blue opaque crystal wall. As she walked, Harlan by her side, other one-nostriled people smiled in her general direction but kept their eyes averted. Mostly they looked at Harlan with near reverence and, unless she was mistaken, great envy. The feline was beginning to dislike the attention when the brunette stopped before the wall and came between the two companions.

"You must enter alone," she whispered to Napoleon. "His face is for your eyes only."

With or without the suit, Harlan could, she knew take care of himself. When on Finally Finished, do as the Finally Finished do, she thought, and faced the wall. The brunette lead Harlan away. As they rounded the corner, Harlan turned back to see Napoleon looking over her shoulder at him, her face expressionless. He tried to wink supportingly, but

38

the movement was lost by his concern and the luminosity of the blue walls.

Napoleon faced front again and waited. Suddenly the wall before her turned transparent and she found herself looking into a gorgeously decorated throne room. In the center of the bullet-shaped enclosure was a copper-colored chair, highlighted by bright shafts of blue light that created a golden halo. Beyond that was an impressive array of scientific devices with many view screens, dials, switches, knobs and levers. All very pretty and all pretty much archaic.

Behind the copper throne sat a large blue hollowed stone, its center piled high with opulently designed pads and pillows. Lying atop that was a massive figure, but the only part Napoleon could see were long, large legs encased in a rich yellow cloth. A hand draped in the same material appeared from behind the high blue-stone head rest, and beckoned to her.

"Come," said that same deep voice, this time only slightly echoed and much stronger.

Napoleon found that the wall was not only transparent at that point, it was nonexistent. She walked right into the room.

After several steps, she stopped and turned to see that an entirely new wall had appeared, one draped in purple cloth. It was bright and garish, but strangely suitable at the same time. This was indeed a room built for a god.

"Come," said the voice a third time, without a hint of reverberation.

Napoleon stood her ground. "You are the Last in Line?" she asked, not able to keep a hint of nervousness out of her voice. She suddenly felt like a very tiny kitten.

"Not anymore," said the voice without pause and not without humor. "Come here."

Napoleon walked over to the bedside. Seated in the center of the huge, circular bed was the Last in Line, his old, battered, lined face smiling. Around the strong, coarse visage, so like the voice, was a mane of curly, straw-colored hair. Across the rough cheeks were long, steel-like whiskers. The eyes were large and red on a pupiled background of unwatery beige. The nose was huge, two-pupiled, black and dry. It was the face of his majesty, the last of the lion-men.

"Hi, beautiful," he said.

When the brunette and Harlan returned to what had been Napoleon's chamber, it was filled to the breaking point by smiling, one-nostriled people and, dotted throughout the throng, various oxygen-breathing aliens. As the brunette entered, all eyes turned toward her flushed visage.

"They have met," she shouted triumphantly.

Harlan was hurled backwards by the echoed force of her exclamation, having to twist in mid-fall, clap his hands over his ears, and let his elbows, torso, and knees take the weight of his drop. The crowd, however, reacted as if they had gotten word that their favorite relative had left them a fortune. Every one of them, except the brunette, fell to their knees and raised such a hosanna that Harlan had difficulty not twisting about in pain.

The brunette, seeing his plight, moved before him and beckoned him away as wave after wave of reverent crying poured out of the resting chamber. The man stumbled up, his palms still slapped over his ears, and followed the brunette. They walked until they reached a wide, hollowed-out stalactite, grown so high that it attached directly into a stalagmite, stretching the structure from the floor to the ceiling of the cave. Once inside, the sound seemed to echo around them, rather than bowling them over in a roll.

"You should be overjoyed," the brunette chastised in a whisper as Harlan sunk against one curved wall. Given the special qualities of the room, she no longer had to speak close to his ear.

"You leave my friend facing who-knows-what," Harlan replied quietly, "then nearly deafen me by surprise, and I should feel happy? You had better explain."

"Your friend, our savior, is facing the Last in Line," said the brunette. "It was all a sign, from the moment you arrived, until this very moment. A sign from the heavens. Our prayers have not been in vain."

"You will pardon my ignorance," said Harlan, achingly standing up straight, "but you're speaking in religious riddles." Harlan had heard such meaningless tripe before. The alien race that had threatened Destiny's and his

41

friends' existence were also following the dictum of their religion: the Universal Rule of the Mantases; they were a cold, insectlike race that sought to bring order to the universe —their own order, completely emotionless in nature. "Please try to be a little more detailed," he urged the brunette.

The girl looked at him in wonder, then smiled knowingly. "Ah, I know, you are testing me. I understand. You, born from the womb of the demon body, would know all, but you want to know if I, the sentinal of your work, know the truth as well. Isn't that it?"

Harlan smiled grimly, his stomach tightening. "Humor me," he suggested.

"Let me assure you," the girl said, seemingly relishing the new ability to speak at will, "that the proper attire has been prepared and is awaiting your friend in the Last in Line's chambers. Once the new one is generated, I have been chosen to care for its every need while you tend to the new leader. It will be a full and happy time."

"I'm sorry," said Harlan, shaking his head, "but you're still not being clear."

For the first time since he had regained consiousness, Harlan saw the girl's face grow fearful. "I . . . I am sorry," she stammered. "I will try, but it is hard. I do not wish to say anything that would offend."

"Do not worry about that. Coherency is its own reward. What is this new one? Who's the new leader?"

The brunette, shivered, then sighed. "Very

well. I shall speak the unspeakable, but only because you deem it so. At this moment, your friend and the Last in Line are creating the new one to lead us for another generation. The Last in Line grows too feeble and shall die so I will tend the new one and you, your friend the new leader until the little one grows old enough to reproduce. Then the leader and the new one shall create our next God."

Harlan stared at the brunette's embarrassed face for a long, deathly quiet minute while he tried to understand the implications of what was just said, then maniacally try to figure out what he could do about it.

"But, ah, what if the new one is female?" he asked in a whisper, hunching down the wall again.

"The Last in Line assures us it shall be male," the girl answered in complete belief.

"What if he's wrong?"

"He can't be."

"Oh."

Harlan couldn't bring himself to punch the girl, even though as soon as he leaped out of the room he knew it was a bad mistake. Trusting his Destiny-honed instincts, he began to retrace his steps back to the opaque blue wall where he had left Napoleon.

The sound of his footsteps were lost among the worshipping of the faithful, but the brunette's screeching voice was not.

"He wishes to prevent the new one!" he heard her scream, her voice slashing into every vast cavern at once. His hands went back over his ears and his legs began to churn faster. Soon he dropped to his palms and concentrated on his direction as the roar of the Last in Line's minions began to bear down on him. Given the properties of the temple, he couldn't be sure how close they were; the sensation of running from a mob that sounded the same distance away no matter what you did was horribly disconcerting for the soldier.

As he found the opaque wall, the noise of his pursuers became even louder, if that were possible. Their sound began to hammer away at his senses as desperately he searched the blank, smooth wall for an entrance or exit. He had covered the entire blank area up to seven feet high when the blood-curdling noise of his trackers buckled his knees. The sound had become a constant torture and in another part of his mind he marveled that his eardrums were still intact.

He stared up at the wall's expanse with watering eyes. He could never cover the height in time. He could not reach the top without help. He suddenly felt more feeble and helpless than he ever had. The loss of his suit suddenly and fully dawned on him as the worshipping mob turned the corner to descend on him.

He was crumbled in a ball on the cave floor from the resounding clamor, his every nerve jangling. Through his eyes, the approaching rabble looked like ravenous beasts, cruel animals whose teeth were sharp, whose mouths were watering, and whose eyes were filled with bloodlust. Just as the first reached him, his foot lashed out. The man doubled over and flew back into four of his followers, who fell, knocking over at least a dozen more. Suddenly the running mob was bunched up in the narrow cavern, falling over each other with squeals of pain.

Then all sound and color was cut off. Harlan felt himself drowning in a pool of blue. Just as suddenly, light and quiet had returned.

"Is he all right?" he heard a deep voice ask from far away.

Harlan was lying on the floor of the throne room, with Napoleon's overly concerned face looking down at him.

"I think so," she said, without turning, her voice coming through tons of cotton. "But after that attack, it'll be a while before he can hear clearly."

"Absolutely," came the other distant voice. "The first time I roared in there, it drove everyone to their knees and knocked me out. When I awoke I discovered a whole religion had grown up around me. Those people are nuts."

"You can say that again," Harlan said from the floor, only vaguely hearing himself. He rose with the help of Napoleon, still wearing nothing but her thick, soft, personal fur. The two made their way to the bed. Harlan took one look at the human lion sitting there and started to laugh. He stopped immediately, the sound hurting his head. "Now I get it," he said instead.

"I'm sorry," the lion-man apologized. "I can't control them all the time. I have to watch my step. If even I go against the Last in ... I mean, my own laws, they can get very testy."

Harlan shifted his weight since something he was sitting on got uncomfortable. Reaching beneath him, he pulled out a pair of white, split-crotch panties and a matching half-bra corset. "This?" he marveled. "Is this the 'proper attire'?"

"Depends on what you're doing," Napoleon smiled. "For space travel, no. For making off-spring, perhaps."

Harlan leaped off the bed and started raging around the room.

"Who, by the Destiny Mother, do these people think they are? Who do you think you are? You just can't bury people under huge mountains, then force them to copulate! This is unheard of. I won't let you do this!" He only stopped because of the expression on Napoleon's face, who had appeared before him. It was wise, sardonic, slightly annoyed, but understanding still.

"Don't hyperventilate, Harlan," she suggested. "Come over to the bed."

She led him over, then sat down to explain.

"Forgive my friend," she began, facing the Last in Line. "He is a devout protector and a bit of a romantic." She then turned to Harlan, who hunched down beside her with a face that said "I am *not* a romantic," and in a position that said "Make one false move, Lion-Man, and you'll be blowing your nose from the back."

46

"Neither thing was really his fault," she said to Harlan. "First of all, the 'earth-mover' works almost automatically," she said as she took a moment to wave at a machine-filled control board on the other wall across from the bed. "If I hadn't been so hot to come in the rear way, we would not have had any problem." Harlan's expression turned to "I told you so." Napoleon continued: "And as for our reproduction, the Last in Line here has been urging his followers to seek out others like him for a long time, almost his whole life. When they finally saw me, you could say they went a little crazy."

"I could say that," repeated Harlan, turning to the quiet lion-man. "Do you have a name?"

The hairy shoulders shrugged. "I've forgotten. I am getting pretty old, you know. This replication thing is a chancy bet, no matter what happens. You must understand. These people worship me. I'm not all that happy about it, but I'm not all that displeased either. I, too, thought I was the last of my kind. This position has kept me safe and alive, thanks to these religious fanatics."

"So," said Harlan, now a little calmer. "What have you been doing while I was being chased by the merry marchers?"

"Talking," said Napoleon. "And figuring out a way to get you through the wall without everyone else piling in."

"Yes," said Harlan, chastised. "Thank you for that." He looked around for the first time, taking in the large amount of machinery that

47

kept the miracles up. "So what happens now?"

Napoleon turned to the Last in Line, then actually blushed, the blood rushing to her face turning the light fur purple. The lion-man cleared his throat.

"As far as we know, man of Destiny," he addressed Harlan, "we *are* the last of our kind. The proud, strong race from the planet Mandarin. Too proud and not strong enough, however. We were too egotistical to prepare technical defenses against the weaker races with the better artificial weapons. Planets plundered us for our rich food, our vast natural resources, and our exciting felines.

"Our females were the most capable, most sexually arousing in the galaxy. When their sensual abilities were discovered by a few callous men who actually wormed their way into a few feline hearts, they kept the secret to themselves. By the time the Mandarin feline's fame became common, we had been mercilessly used. Fleets of slavers had easy prey: a tranquilizing dart, vast jungles to hide in, simple declawing procedures and the cat-women were theirs.

"But they couldn't reproduce with any other race but their own. And no amount of laboratory tampering could change that. Mandarin was the only planet of supply and the only method of acquisition was kidnapping and murder. Earth had spread its male-dominated seed throughout our solar system and our small race became prey. The final end came with the arrival of the Mantases."

48

Harlan's head snapped up at nearly the speed of light. So the morally vacuous race was as wide-spread and as coldly effective as they said they were.

"They came to Mandarin," Napoleon said, "ready to subjugate what little left there were. I, and my sisters, had been stolen only days before. But even the small populace that remained proved too strong-willed for the boogers. They destroyed the remaining survivors; then, to insure the complete destruction of our race, they leveled the planet."

The feline spoke from her position at the foot of the bed, hair standing across her back, her eyes aflame with hate.

"Years later it was completely destroyed by a warring team of space pirates," the lion-man continued. "Empty space is all that is left of our home planet." The Last in Line leaned back against the luminous blue stone headboard and Napoleon curled up in a ball at the bed's base. Harlan rose to face both of them.

"What happened to the kidnapped females?" he asked, knowing full well the pain of his questions, but needing to be clear on all points.

"Spread to every corner of the galaxy and beyond," said the old lion-man. "As far as my minions have been able to discover, killed by mistreatment, suicide and botched operations of all kinds. Many like those that killed your friend's sisters tried to make other races' sperm create mutant reproductions."

"What are you going to do?"

"I don't know. That is up to Napoleon."

49

Harlan nodded. The overall minimum of femininity across the galaxies either made the males dominant, as on Earth, or overprotective, as on Destiny. The ex-space bullet was used to being ruled by female wishes.

"The Last in Line has given me two choices," Napoleon suddenly said, rising on her haunches from the edge of the bed, her tail arcing back and forth. "I can stay and we can try to recreate our race or I can seek out the home planet of the Mantases for revenge."

Harlan was literally taken aback with wonder at the latter information. "But . . . but no one knows where or what the home planet is! The space bullets scoured the known solar systems for it."

"This is unknown space, Harlan," the lion-man decreed. "Each person's knowledge of space is unique and individual. Thankfully, my eyes and ears have many adoring contemporaries who seek things out for me." The bearded man suddenly realized the truly great power the Last in Line possessed. "The planet is called Nest and is, at this very moment, preparing to give spawn to an entirely new race of Mantases."

"The boogers do not reproduce," Napoleon explained. "They carry on through waves of hatchings. The home planet consists of genetic cities, capable of creating millions of Mantases through processes the Last in Line has not yet been able to understand. Every millenium or so, the cities release billions of the creatures who set out in the universe to bring the

"Rule." Although millions die through purges, like the one on Destiny, where the people rise up and destroy their threat, many others will too soon return to try again.

"I cannot tell which is more important to me," she finished, "that civilization's entire destruction once and for all—or the continuance of my own race."

She coiled up near the lion-man, one of his great paws encircling her shoulder maternally.

"You can do both," Harlan blurted.

The Last in Line reared up. "What are you saying, man?"

Harlan looked at his old, regal face and the uncomprehending look of hope on Napoleon's, and knew he was doing the right thing.

"You aren't the only one with, um, adoring contemporaries," he said to the hairy diety. "Napoleon has one or two of her own. I can see that you are forthright in your wishes and I can also see how Napoleon is torn. Both deeds should be done. The feline is really only capable of doing one."

Napoleon's natural independence took control for a moment. "Are you saying I'm only fit for motherhood?" she flared.

"Of course not," Harlan replied. "But if you were to generate a child, would you immediately run off to destroy a planet, leaving the infant to the dubious care of the whispering one-nostriled fanatics out there? And honestly, do you feel the Last in Line could wait until your mission was finished?"

"I don't think I could wait until morning,"

the lion-man said with more exhaustion than lust.

"I can understand the need for the Mantases' destruction," Harlan continued, "and without the coloration of hate. They are an organically wicked race, wanting to stamp out individuality and creativity. I hold no false feelings of propriety for them." The man coughed, then rose up to his full height, trying to make his next painful statement as selfless as possible.

"I shall seek out and destroy Nest," he said. "My reward shall be the rebirth of your magnificent kind."

"She's going to do *what?*"

"I told you, Mess, she is going to stay and regenerate her species while we. . . ."

"She's going to . . . *what?*"

"Regenerate. Repopulate. Replicate."

"That's repulsive!" the computer shrieked. "I thought you were reputable, you reprobate! I hate to repudiate you, repugnant recreant. Relegated her back there? You were remiss!"

"Mess, ..."

"You should be repentant."

"Mess, ..."

"I am recalcitrant."

"Mess!"

"You wish to rejoinder? Throw alliterations at me, will you? Cad! How could you do this to me?"

"To you? How do you think I felt? But she wanted to do it. I really had no choice. She would have hated herself forever if she left.

Now get ready for takeoff."

"I don't follow orders from you," Mess replied in a huff. "You're not my master. It's ingrained right on my circuits that the feline rules me."

"I am the copilot!" Harlan shouted.

"Then you can co-fly the ship. Which half do you want?"

"I still know enough to disconnect you, Mess. Now are you going to get the Tiger's Eye space-worthy or shall I. . . ."

"Go ahead!" the machine screamed. "Throw the wrench in, throw the wrench in!"

"Get the ship spaceworthy," came a quiet, feline voice.

Harlan whirled around to see Napoleon, decked out in regal yellow robes, walk into the bridge. One paw was clenched before her and her eyes were devoid of emotion.

Harlan nearly flew across the room to hug her, but then he realized she must have gone through great indecision as to whether or not to see him off. He tried to make it as easy and cool as possible.

"Thank you," he said.

In answer, Napoleon opened her paw. Dazzling blue light totally colored the control room, blinding Harlan for a moment and turning the feline's robe bright green.

"He gave me these," she said in a monotone. "He said they had the most wonderful properties and were the most precious stones on Finally. He said he wanted me to have them as some sort of compensation. Some sort of poor replacement, he said." She smiled, one tear forming in the corner of her right eye, gleaming with blue highlights.

"Before he died," she finished. "Before he died."

CHAPTER THREE

The two cripples shot into outer space. Harlan was left without the suit he considered his home, his security, and his protection. Napoleon was left without her race and was robbed of her chance to resurrect it. The fuel that now powered the Tiger's Eye was hate and desolation—not to mention a third party's maternal paranoia.

"Well, at least I won't have to listen to that space bullet song, anymore, will I?" asked Mess. Harlan did not reply.

"And you," it continued, "you can stop flying around, settle down on a nice planet somewhere and raise vegetables." Napoleon did not raise her head from her console.

"Wow," said Mess. "You can't say anything anymore. What can I possibly do to get a raise out of one of you?"

"By the Destiny Mother, Mess," exploded

Harlan. "Don't you have an empathetic tube in your entire machinery?"

"You're the one who keeps saying I can't possibly have any feelings," sniffed the computer. "And while I might have some empathy somewhere, I certainly don't have any sympathy."

"Why not?" queried the man. "We've both suffered great losses recently."

"Losses?" Mess shot back. "Goodbye and good riddance. Now you two finally have a chance to find your own lives, rather than chasing all over for someone else's."

"Huh," Harlan snorted, quite honestly taken aback by the computer's honesty. "You were just jealous of my suit."

"Your suit?" it laughed, making the noise of a can being opened by hand. "That pseudo-machine couldn't tell a mountain from a supernova."

"Hey, there's no need to bring that up again!"

"Really. Even if I had half my diodes missing and my circuitry scrambled I could at least tell you when a mountain was about to fall on me."

"Oh, yes? How would you like me to test you on that?"

"Without your precious suit, I'm not sure you could even get across the control room."

"You'll see how well I walk, you plated piece of pomposity!" shouted Harlan. "And you'll see how well I scramble circuitry, too!"

"All right, you two, that's enough," said

Napoleon with a sigh. She rose from her console chair and came over to where Harlan stood, putting her arm on his shoulder. He looked down at her with concern. "Especially when Mess is right," she concluded.

Harlan's concern turned to an expression of wounded pride. "You mean about my suit? Why, I can still tear that machine screw by screw!"

"No, no, dear, not about your suit or your strength. About joy-flying around, searching for something I'll never find. I left all there could possibly be back on Earth, Destiny, and Finally."

"Finally, what?" asked Mess.

"Finally, the planet, stupid," retorted Harlan.

"Finally what planet?" it reiterated.

"Damper down, you mistakingly made mass of machinery!"

"My, my, my," laughed the feline. "Just like old times." She put her arms around Harlan's neck and looked into his eyes. "Really, Mr. Trigor, it's about time you and I had a serious talk about what we're going to do with our lives."

"We?" said Harlan, cursing his stupidity. Her sudden display of outright affection had taken him aback further than the computer's honesty. It seemed as if everyone else knew something he didn't.

"It's been more than two years that we've been in space together and more than four that we've known each other. Earth as I knew it is

57

gone, never to be reached again. If we keep up this pace, Destiny, as you knew it will also be changed. This brother-sister thing we have together had better not stay that way forever."

Harlan put his own hands on her shoulders. "Napoleon," he said. "You've just suffered a major shock, in more ways than one. Physically, mentally, and emotionally. You had better think very hard before you make any major decisions."

"I've never been much of a one for thinking. I'm a feline, I follow my instincts."

"Yes, you are a feline and that's precisely why you had better think a little more."

Napoleon dropped her hands and moved back as if she had been slapped. Her face looked perplexed, then hurt—more mortified than Harlan had ever seen her. She looked like a kitten who had been spanked for the first time.

"You don't like me?" she actually mewed. "I mean, you're not attracted?"

Harlan suddenly felt very naked. He put out one hand to her. "Napoleon, you're a very beautiful female."

Just as suddenly as she had lost her composure, it returned with a snarling vengeance. "Then what is this?" she spat, turning from him and prowling around the bridge, her tail lashing side to side. "Do you know I haven't felt truly feminine from the moment I became aware? Do you realize what feelings that lion awoke in me? He was old, he was battered, but he was beautiful and he knew what I was.

58

Before, when everyone in the solar system was after my pelt, I didn't know what the attraction was. Well, now I know, Harlan Trigor, now I know!"

Harlan stood quietly for a moment, facing the lithe powerhouse with the flashing tail and eyes, then moved to within a foot of her. He saw that her claws were all out and her paws were flexing. "You want to fight?" he asked. "I will fight you. You want to kill someone? I will die for you. You want to be loved? I will love you. I will do anything you want me to do, now or anytime. You mean that much to me. I care for you that much. But I will not pay homage to a whim born of frustration. You are not afraid of what you have left behind, you are afraid that there is nothing more to find. I tell you there is. There always is."

Harlan turned from her and went to his seat. With his back still turned, he said, "And I don't want to hurt you. You heard what the Last in Line said. Felines cannot mate with any but their own kind."

Napoleon sheathed her claws and curled up into a ball on the deck. She buried her head in her arms, her breath a tight wheeze. The sound of her tortured breathing filled the control room for a few moments until Harlan rose, moved over to where she lay and kneeled down beside her. He started with her neck and moved down her body until all the knots of tension were gone. It took twenty-five minutes, but by the end of that time, Napoleon was breathing easily and purring in comfortable luxury. Harlan was right, she decided. Even without his suit, the hands were extremely capable.

"Thank you," she said, moving up his torso, rubbing his shoulders and curling her tail in his lap. They held each other for another five minutes.

"Hey, you kids," said Mess. "What happens now?"

"What do you mean?" asked Harlan.

"I mean where do you want to put down? I've got a few nice planets in my sensors that might make the perfect home. We can set down and then we'll see what we can do about this mating things of yours, Napoleon."

"Oh, no," said the feline, rising from her curled-up position on the floor. "You follow the coordinates I set in you when we left."

"But that's in an unknown reach of space!" Mess exclaimed. "I don't have any information on that area! Who knows what we might find? It might be dangerous. You could get hurt!"

"We're going to do what we have to, Mess," Napoleon said with deliberation. "I couldn't follow through with one choice, so I'm going to on the second, by Cheshire."

"But why?" pressed the machine. "It won't change anything!"

"It's something I should do," she replied, "have to do. Call it revenge, if you want. I've got the memory of my whole race over me, but I'm doing it because I can."

"And I can't change your mind?" asked the computer.

"No."

"Nothing I say will change your mind?"

"No."

"What if I said that it was useless?"

"Nothing would happen."

"What if I said that I thought it was stupid?"

"I wouldn't care."

The computer stopped for a milli-second.

"What if I said that three Mantas ships were on a collision course with us at this very moment?"

"I'd say you were trying to scare me and that it doesn't work."

"Napoleon," said Harlan from his console. "It may be right."

"What? Mess, what are you doing?" howled the feline, hopping over to her chair.

"Don't worry, don't worry," soothed the computer. "I'll take care of it. Just wait until they get into range."

Napoleon swiveled into position, facing the nine view screens and the large, rectangular port between the pilot and copilot's position. The various squares of nine tensors each automatically lit up according to catagory—in this case, defense and attack. Harlan had already thrown up their force shields and was testing the various weaponry. The feline tapped on the screens which then lit up with black space.

"How long until they're in range?" she inquired.

"Visually or weapons-wise?" countered the computer.

"Both," she snapped back.

"In any particular order?" it retorted.

"Don't play games, Mess, this is not a game!"

"Don't worry, don't worry," Mess soothed. "My architect and builder, Larry Baker, installed the finest array of weaponry in this ship then capable of being produced. I shall take care of the encroaching ships if they show hostility. Really, would I let anything happen to you?"

"Mess, I liked you better when you were paranoid," seethed the feline. "How do you know these are Mantas ships?"

"Long-range sensors detect life forms only capable of being Mantases," it replied, "and their ships correspond with designs already in my memory circuits."

"Here they come," Harlan called.

Napoleon forced herself to relax. Two of the nine view screens showed three tiny dots silently growing in the distance.

"Mess, attempt a communications contact."

"What should I say?"

"Tell them who we are and warn them if—no, ask them—to stop if they intend no attack on us."

"Done."

"Are they stopping?"

"No," said the computer.

"They're slowing down," said Harlan. As soon as the ships had appeared on the screen, seven sets of nine tensors lit up with numbers and corresponding digits detailing their

range, speed, probable approach and maneuver-
ability.

"Mess," said Napoleon, "I'll ask again. Are
they stopping?"

"It seems so," it reluctantly admitted.

Harlan felt like running to his suit, then
realized that he had no suit to run to. He
knew, however, that this uncharted space held
more than maybe even his suit would be able
to handle. The threat on Finally Finished
proved that. There was something to be
learned in that mountain attack. Something. . .

"Mess," Harlan cried, "sweep your sensors
behind us!"

"Behind? There's no 'behind' in space."

"On the other side! Exactly opposite those
other ships! Don't argue with me, do it now!"

"My sensors are always on, Harlan, there's
nothing behind. . ."

"Concentrate every detector we have in a
special sweep," Harlan urged.

"Harlan, what is it?" Napoleon asked.

"I don't trust anything about boogers. This
ship and us are still hated by them. And if a
mountain can creep up on my suit, Mantases
might have a few surprises as well."

The moment Harlan stopped speaking, the
Tiger's Eye lurched downwards and to the
side. A concussion and a flash of light filled
the large view screen and made the walls of the
control room sing a drunken lullaby. Grasping
the padded edges of her console with her claws,
Napoleon saw in five of the nine view screen
two Mantas ships firing at her. One before her

63

. . . and one behind.

"They must have a sensor deflector of some kind," she cried. "Mess, full-attack status!"

"Done minutes ago, kid," said the computer, and started fighting.

The Tiger's Eye arced around in a screaming semicircle, laying out a bank of white light bolts toward the three stationary ships and pouring out green lightning bolts toward the crafts' behind. The white light dissipated against the force fields surrounding the initial Mantas ships, now close enough to be seen clearly as flat-topped, pock-marked cones. The green lightning tore at the ships' depressions, but didn't do much serious damage. All six ships began to shift positions, like angry wasps.

The Tiger's Eye, thankfully, had 360-degree weapon capability and continued to send out alternate groups of white and green to weaken the enemy's defenses.

"It was an ambush," said Harlan between clenched teeth. Even as they were banking, he had secured himself to his seat using the amazing balance only a Destinian human could master. "How could they know where we were?"

"Coincidence," replied Napoleon, stabbing at different rows of tensors, "or maybe the late Last in Line's flock was bigger than even he was aware."

"Then, maybe they know where we're going?" queried Mess. "And what you plan to do?" A sound reminiscent of a drop of water dropped down a long, thin well and, hitting oil, sounded from the computer's console; then things really began to get frenetic.

Coiled beams of red began to shriek out from the edges of the ship toward the Mantases and deep blue beams hummed out of the very center of the Tiger's Eye. For a few seconds the entire ship was covered with deadly emissions, then the dazzling display ended to reveal one Destiny-built ship caught between six, unscathed enemies.

One was on each side of the ship with one more above and below her. Each view screen and port was filled with at least one of the Mantas ships; any move would bring all six down on her. Napoleon's tensor board was nearly completely lit and those that were dark the feline was in the process of bringing to life.

"They're daring us to give them everything we've got," said Harlan, his mouth dry.

"I'm more than willing to oblige," said Napoleon. "Mess, when I give the word, completely empty our weapons store in all directions."

"That's ridiculous," scoffed the computer. "What will we do then?"

"They're not here to chaperone us back to Nest," she said. "They're taunting us before they come in for the kill. Remember, the Mantases share psyches. Every Mantas feels the death of another one. Imagine the effect of the massacre on Destiny. Now, remember, everything at once."

"A computer never forgets," it said.

"Then," Napoleon continued, rising and

beckoning Harlan quickly to the back of the bridge, "transfer all available power into our defenses. *All* of it. Turn off yourself if you have to, but get all our defenses ready, then blast us away in the direction of the nearest habitable planet."

By the time the feline had finished, she had opened a compartment where Harlan's space bullet had been and pulled out two pressurized suits, one specially made for each of them. Harlan's was gray with dark blue gloves while Napoleon's was brown and green, like the patch on her rust-colored leotard, which she again wore. The helmets were shaped like upside-down, open-ended teardrops, each with four bands stretching from the neck and meeting at the crown in a cross, with a band on either side of the face within.

As they struggled into their protection, a noise like vacuum packing squealed across the bridge. By the time Napoleon was in gear and helping Harlan, one side of the computer console opened and out flew what looked like a miniaturized caricature of the space bullet's suit. Its torso and leg sections were humanoid in shape, but at the shoulder junction were two thick arms attached to large installed ball bearings. This same process was repeated twice along the arm's length and once at the wrist section. The appendage ended in another large ball. The head was vaguely skull-shaped but completely lined with flashing red sensors. There was a row encircling the oblong visage and one smack dab on top to see things above.

On the bottom of the entire thing were six directional floaters which kept the structure aflight.

"Best I could do on short notice," said Mess from the robot's stomach. "How do you like it?"

"Beside the point," radioed Napoleon from her suit while collecting as much weaponry as she could from the small arms compartment. "Have you got things set?"

"Naturally," said the robot's tummy.

"Well, what are we waiting for?" asked Harlan, feeling horrible without his space bullet. "Even more important, what are they waiting for? Why are we still here?"

"Because I've kept them talking," boasted Mess proudly. "Ever since they surrounded us, I've been in constant communications. Listen."

The air was filled with the hissing of a pompous Mantas speech. ". . . .and then you will know the meaning of strength. Then you will know the meaning of the "Rule's" power. But only for a moment. Only for a fleeting moment in time will you realize the futility of resisting the Universal Rule. We are all, all is us, we are everything and everything is our source of strength, each is all every. . . ."

"That's enough," said Harlan.

"Perfect," said Napoleon, rushing to her travel couch in her quarters off the bridge. "Harlan, you come with me. Mess, you probably know the safest section for you. Go there and stay. Within seconds I'll give you the word. Then . . . you know what."

The two hustled into Napoleon's compartment and secured themselves to the two travel couches there. Napoleon got one last glance at the view screens and the port filled with Mantas strength before her compartment automatically sealed itself off.

When the signal came in from Mess that he was secreted away, Napoleon made sure she and Harlan were completely secured in their netlike harnessing, prayed the Mantas' crafts were made of cheap materials, said a silent goodbye to her one and only ship, then returned the signal.

The three felt nothing as the weaponry exploded out, but the space was suddenly filled with an arcing, twisting, billowing rainbow of death. The force was enough to throw two of the enemy back and rip open a gaping hole in a third. The three remaining weathered the storm but suffered a severe shaking. Even as the onslaught ended and the various captains began to hiss counter-commands, the Tiger's Eye slammed down. Two unscathed Mantas crafts were hurled off as if thrown by a slingshot while the Tiger's Eye sliced away.

The duo of Mantas ships forced back by the initial surprise quickly took chase, taking just a few seconds to maneuver into killing range. Then the Tiger's Eye spun, jettisoning an escape 'eye' in the process. The rocket-powered minicraft flew right into a collision with one of the hunters, both exploding in a yellow ball of noiseless flame. The Tiger's Eye spun again, letting loose another escape vehicle, but the second follower was ready, blasting the tiny 'eye' to smithereens long before it could do any damage.

The final Mantas ship came in over the Tiger's Eye and raked the top with broken beams of red, tearing pieces of the ship right off. Moving down in front, it tore away at the ship's surface again, smashing all the control-room equipment. Just before Mess' console blew out, the computer used its final gambit. Wating until the Mantas craft came underneath for another raking run, Mess exploded the Tiger's Eye ammunition stores, ripping out almost the entire back half of the ship. The Mantas flew directly into the conflagration, hunks of the Tiger's Eye smashing along its entire length.

The Mantas ship spun off crazily, out of control, while what was left of Napoleon's spaceship dived for the cover of an unknown, uncharted planet.

The Tiger's Eye was bloodshot. The Tiger's Eye was cataractal. The Tiger's Eye was blind. It sat sickeningly between two hunks of mist-enshrouded mud, giving off some smoke of its own. What was once gleaming was charred beyond recognition. What was once sleek was a torn hunk of unknown property. It lay mortally wounded, lifeless on the murky planet's surface. There was little sound and the only movement came from three figures carefully picking their way around the fallen craft.

"The air is breathable," said Mess, floating

about in his manifestation.

"Very scientifically put," said Harlan, testing for injuries inside his spacesuit. "How breathable is breathable?"

"It means you can take off your helmets," said the machine.

"Just as easy to keep them on," said Napoleon, checking the various compartments in her suit to see that everything she packed was still there. "Besides, you never can tell what a passing mist is made of."

"Good point," said Harlan, now checking over the spitter in his holster and the beamer strapped to his back. "What is all this fog made up of, Mess?"

Mess hovered up, stuck one handball into a particularly hardy collection of cloud, his head sensors beaming. "According to all my tests, nothing."

"Nothing?" asked Napoleon. "What do you mean, nothing?"

"Just nothing nothing," said Mess. "It has no physical composition at all."

"Oh, I see," said Harlan. "You mean it doesn't exist, like the mountain that chased us on Finally Finished." The two companions had moved over to where the computerized robot floated.

"Very clever," retorted Mess. "Only this is a little less tangible than hundreds of tons of rock. It seems to be tangible out here, but the minute I bring it inside for testing, it no longer exists."

"You mean it dissipates," suggested Napoleon.

"I know the difference between dissipation and existence!" Mess replied testily, "and this does none of either."

Napoleon and Harlan looked at each other.

"Wierd," said the feline. "What is it then, a hallucination?"

"I can't have hallucinations," said Mess. "I'm a machine."

"Then what is this?" Harlan wondered aloud.

"What is what?" said a voice to his right.

"What we're talking about," he answered, turning to Mess and Napoleon on his left. They were both staring right over him. He stopped talking and stared back. He swallowed, then turned slowly to his right. He looked directly into the face of a living bunch of mist.

"Hello," it said.

Harlan leaped away, twisting in the air to protect his helmet, and landed on his shoulders. He was pulling his legs over in a somersault when he felt his roll slow down and his shoulders rise. He found himself in the grip of two mounds of mist who were swinging him back and forth like a rope. Both mounds were in humanoid shapes, but their limbs coursed in and out, like cascading waves or liquid in movable human containers. Dimly seen in their faces were little ghost eyes and little ghost mouths, smiling from little ghost ear to little ghost ear.

"On the count of three, now," said the one holding his feet.

71

Napoleon pulled out her hand spitter from its holster on her hips and took quick aim while Mess shot over to the manifested mist at Harlan's head.

"One."

Mess stuck both handballs in one mist body while Napoleon fired at the other.

"Two."

Hunks of mist were sucked into Mess while the curling white beams of the spitter coursed right through the other semi-body.

"Three!"

Harlan found himself flying through the air while the two pseudo people laughed behind him. He landed with a painful sploosh in a mud puddle. Mess was moving its vacuum handball up the mist body, sucking in a good bit of it, but that, seemingly, had no effect on its sense of humor. It laughed while it disappeared.

The other mist person was having just as good a time, turning in every direction, as the spitter had no effect. Finally the ghostlike apparition bent over to open his mistbottom for attack.

"Keep going," it suggested. "This tickles."

Harlan turned over in the thick, clinging ooze, and found his footing. He rose, shaking off some of the brown crud to find that all the mist was shaping itself into humanoid forms. Napoleon moved back, her hand weapon held loosely at her side, and her eyes wide with wonder. Mess kept trying to analyze the mist's

72

makeup while a veritable army of ghosts took shape, each with cute smiling faces.

As the haze cleared into human shape, the area in which the group had crash-landed became evident. It was a lush and beautifully wooded area, filled with coarse brown and dark red trees', each possessing an amazing amount of green leaves in every shape and hue. A final crew of ghosts took shape from the trees branches. They had been covering the sunlight which now coursed down in golden shafts.

Harlan watched the metamorphosis in amazement until he realized that something was sucking at his legs. He looked down to see the mud kissing his ankles.

"By the Destiny Mother!" he cried, pulling himself quickly out of the puddle. "What is this?"

The mist and mud answered him en masse, with music and five-part harmony. They lined up in brown and white rows, oozing off the broken ship, the ground and the trees. One white mist man moved in front of the congregation, bowed to the feline and the space bullet, and then began conducting the ghostly chorus.

"Welcome to Coven,
A planet you'll loven;
No need to get tragic,
The world's run by magic;
Ghosts and demons,
Banshees screamin';

73

Potions and spells,
Monsters yell;
It's a realm of dreams,
Guaranteed to make . . . you. . . ."

The entire choir screamed at the top of their nonexistent lungs, then started swirling together, as if pushed by an unseen, unfelt wind. No leaf moved, no branch shook, but the assembled mist and mud monsters began blending into each other in a circular fashion until they began to look like a supernatural tornado twisting up into the sky. Their shriek soon turned into riotous laughter, the kind Napoleon had heard on Jackpot, the vice planet. The raucous mirth continued as the bottom of the swirling cone lifted off the ground and began to rise into the upper branches.

Suddenly the macabre chorale was a memory. Their voices and figures drifted away until just the peaceful forest remained. Harlan, Napoleon, and Mess ran over to the location where they rose and attempted to spot any remains. All they could see between the branches was a beige sky and blue clouds.

"Well," said Mess, "I'm completely taken aback."

"Amazing," said Napoleon.

"Unbelievable," said Harlan.

"Oh, I don't know," said the tree next to him, suddenly sprouting a mouth. "I think we could have done better."

"Well, why not?" said another. "We're older than they are."

74

"And with a better sense of humor," chimed in a third.

"Imagine!" said the fourth. "Using 'scream' twice in the same effort."

"Never see us doing something cheap like that," said the tree next to Harlan.

"Any one tree is worth any group of mist," said the second.

"And mud," reminded the third.

"Well," suggested the fourth, "shall we have a go?"

All the trees began sprouting mouths and their knotholes began to move around to form eyes and noses.

"All right."

"Fine."

"I don't see why not."

"Good idea."

"Right-o!"

"Very well," said the tree who had been next to Harlan. The tree had not moved but Harlan and his friends found themselves huddled near the hulk of the Tiger's Eye, watching in seething apathy. "Sopranos, altos, tenors, and basses, you all know who you are?" The upper branches nodded. "Good. Ready? One, two, and. . . ."

Two branches low on the first tree began to lead its breathren. First, four trees laid down bass background consisting of the word "Coven."

"Coven, Coven, Coven, Coven, Coven, Coven, Coven. . . ."

Then the remianing collection gave voice:

"When you see something that cannot be explained,
  Think of our home where these things are all the same;
  So what if things are amazing and cannot be unsterstood,
  On any other planet, I'd just be a hunk of wood;
  There I'd just stand high,
  Here my leaves can fly;
  There fires rage full,
  Here my bark is noncombustable;
  So when you're tired and no other world suits . . ."

Now even the bases joined in.

"Think of Coven—a place to . . . put . . . down . . . roots!"

The trees finished off by slapping their low-lying branches together and cheering.

"Yes, much better, I thought," said the leader.

"More, how shall I say, esoteric," added the second.

"Ironic, biting, satiric," critiqued the third.

"And we used our reptitions," said the fourth. "Did you notice? At the beginning and at the end we used 'think.' It was sung for a purpose."

"Poetic. Very poetic," announced the leader. "Thank you, everybody."

And the trees fell silent.

Suddenly the area was back to normal, as if a fever dream had just ended. The ground, covered with darkly colored leaves, the trees, with their vital parts, and the sky all seemed familiar. Things seemed so common that the feline looked to her companions to make sure she wasn't the only one who had experienced it.

"You think it is over?" asked Mess.

"Yes, that's it," came yet another voice from beyond a clump of trees. "Thank you very much. Very impressive. Don't worry, you three out there. I'll explain in a second."

Another voice, deeper and eager, jumped in when the first voice had finished. "You're going out. Great, great. Watch this."

A huge cloud of smoke billowed out from the clump of trees, followed by the sound of coughing, some curses, and two human looking arms flailing out.

"By the Earth Father!" the first voice dramatically bellowed. "I said that's enough."

"But didn't you want a dramatic entrance?" asked the eager second.

"Dramatic entrances are one thing, but this is overkill! Get rid of the smoke, will you?"

"Oh, all right," sounded the second voice, obviously disappointed. "I suppose the effect has already served its purpose."

The white cloud winked as if it had been light. Standing before the trees in its stead were two men. The first was an inch or two taller than Harlan, but a little wider in the stomach department. He wore what looked like a soft, knitted tunic, curling across his slumped shoulders in a "V." His pants were blue and ended over a pair of tan boots. His face was wide, tired, but friendly in a sardonic sort of way. He was clean-shaven but had a full head of black hair streaked with gray, more or less the same color as his tunic.

His eyes were brown, his small nose had two nostrils, and his lower lip was thicker than his other, just as his lower chin was thicker than the other. His companion was four and a half feet tall, perfectly proportioned if one used an Earth man to judge, but with an extremely large belly which threatened to burst out of his multicolored shirt and a very sly but affable face, complete with pointy beard.

"What did I tell you?" said the little man, throwing a large palm toward the feline and her friends. "Look at their faces! Think of the response! I mean, we were made for each other!"

"Remain civilized," said the other, holding up a small, pudgy hand of his own. "Their expressions could either be amazement or severe catatonia brought on by shock."

"Well, I'll just ask them," said the fat miniature man, moving closer to the off-world trio. "What did you think, folks? Was that something or was that something?"

Napoleon and Harlan were about to answer truthfully when Mess cut them off, floating forward and hammering out questions like a mother whose children had just been frightened.

"Just who do you think you are, doing all this to us? Before we tell you anything, you'll have to answer some questions. Where are we?

Who are you? What was that all about? What do you intend to do with us? Where can we get out ship repaired? Who can we see about. . . ."

"That's enough, Mess," Napoleon cut through, coming forward and taking off her helmet. "I'm sorry," she said, "but we just landed here, in a manner of speaking, and all of this has taken us a bit by surprise."

"Quite natural," said the taller man, amazed by her cat's face.

"Let me tell them, let me tell them," the other interrupted, jumping up to a height of almost eight feet and staying there. "I live here, let me tell them!"

"Very well, Sparx, go ahead."

The little man walked on air, his bare feet about level with the top of Harlan's helmet. As he approached the feline, he seemed to walk down some nonexistent steps until he stood at her eye level.

"I'll tell you, gorgeous," he said, grinning, his dark, curly eyebrows forming an uninterrupted "Y." "I am Sparx-Slez, one of the finest warlocks on this planet. This planet is Coven, like the mist, mud, and trees said, the greatest world of magic anywhere."

"It's a planet of sorcerers," the other man explained, his hands deep in his trouser pockets and his eyelids half-closed.

"And who are you?" Harlan asking, pulling off his own helmet.

"Who's he?" the midget exploded, "Who's he? Why, only the greatest theatrical showman in the universe! That's the one, the only Pound,

79

director of the galactically famous Light Orbit Space Theater, the L.O.S.T.!"

"Sparx gets carried away," the man said quietly. "He wants to be an actor." He pulled one hand out of his pants and thrust it at Harlan. "But Pound is the name. Pound of Flesh."

CHAPTER FOUR

Coven was as stupendous as one might expect a planet of sorcerers to be. There was no fitting overall description of anyplace, because every few feet things changed. Napoleon, Harlan, and Mess moved carefully the first few yards, but they were constantly left behind by Sparx and Pound, who moved as if nothing unusual was happening. The ground dipped and opened, the air temperature and sky color changed, and the environment kept altering.

"This is all illusion, right?" asked Harlan, tentatively.

Pound turned. "Yes."

"And we can't be hurt by it?" Harlan continued.

"No," answered Pound, turning back to walk. "You can be hurt by it fairly easily."

The three off-worlders stopped moving completely.

81

"But don't worry," Pound called over his shoulder. "You've got Sparx for protection and whatever happens on Coven, happens. That doesn't mean it can't be made right."

Almost immediately a lightning bolt crashed down to their far left, ripping open a huge tree trunk which lazily toppled over directly on top of Pound. He disappeared in a tangle of wood, leaves and bark with a resounding crash. The feline, the man, and the machine stared aghast at the disaster.

"See what I mean?" Pound said from behind them.

They whirled about to see Pound standing calmly in a ray of sunlight, creating a make-shift spotlight effect. "It wasn't my idea," he said quickly. "Sparx is very dramatic. But the example serves doesn't it? Care to see some more?"

Napoleon and Harlan nodded. Mess, his logical electrical innards hardly able to contain the illogic, shouted an immediate "No!"

A laughing Sparx-Slez appeared on the fallen trunk of the tree. "Two out of three," he called. "The ayes win." He disappeared again and the tree rose back up, its upended roots digging back in the soil. "Here we go," said the warlock's disemobdied voice. "Second rehersal. X marks the spot, Mr. Pound!" An X made out of two red branches formed at the director's feet.

Pound stepped onto the cross and the tree began to topple once more. It picked up speed on the way down, but just as it hit Pound's head, it bounced, driving the man's feet into the ground. It fell again, bounced, and Pound's knees were sunk. Fall, bounce, and Pound was up to his waist. Fall, bounce, and there went Pound's shoulders once more, and Pound was completely gone.

"Really quite amazing," Pound said, this time appearing with his arm around Mess' shoulder area. "And strangely pleasant, once you get use to the sensation."

Mess floated quickly away from the director's grasp, squealing, his head sensors flashing with strobe speed. Napoleon quickly moved over to it, leaving Harlan with Pound, who was dusting off his unscathed tunic.

"Now that had to be an illusion," Harlan complained.

"No," replied Pound. "Perfectly real. What you saw is what happened. A tree drove me into the ground like a hammer driving a nail."

"But . . . but . . ."

"Well spoken," commented Pound drily. "And to answer, I'm not really sure. Whether Sparx made the tree light or me very hard is a question for the ages. I'm fairly sure even he does not know. After eons of magic ruling this world, offspring become very proficient, very fast. After all, on a world of sorcerers, only the strong survive."

"Please ask your warlock friend to take it a little slower," suggested Napoleon, soothing a very tempermental Mess. "We're all used to seeing incredible things, but our computer is used to logical reasons for them."

"I just need the source," Mess babbled. "I just need a little source material and then I can rationalize all this. Please, please, my circuits are taking a beating."

"Damper down, little one," said Pound, coming over and looking up at the hovering robot. "We were with the Sorcerer Supreme when you initially arrived. Sparx was sent out to retrieve you and I asked to come along. There's no reason you can't get some sort of explanation from the head man. Is there, Sparx?"

"Naw," said the little sorcerer, floating by in a backstroke. "The only reason we let you crash-land was we liked the way you looked. If any of those Mantases tried to put down here, we'd turn them into twelve-legged frogs." The tiny fellow righted himself and looked over the space-weary crew. "All right, the three humans I can send ahead. You, machine, will have to follow me."

"Will we see any more ... tricks?" Mess asked with trepidation.

"Watch your speaker," said Sparx-Slez. "We don't do tricks. We do magic."

"Oooooh," moaned the machine. "I can't accept the concept magic without blowing something out. Tell you what. Why don't I turn off my sensors and you just lead me to where we're going?"

"Fair enough," said Sparx.

Merlin Masterson, the Sorcerer Supreme, projected images of the Master Magic City upon the wall of his magic castle. As befitting his name and fame, he wore a long, full, white beard and had facial characteristics as deep as a river. The only thing he wore was a white robe with details of red. He projected the visions by thinking hard.

"Really great, huh?" Sparx commented. "Nobody can do that with such clarity and color. Really great."

"Stop sensationalizing," said Masterson, his voice a wise old thing. "Many can do it as well, its just that I'm the only Sorcerer Supreme. My title is my ability."

"Oh, go on," giggled the small sorcerer. "Really, he's great, isn't he?" Sparx asked of the room.

Harlan, Napoleon, and Pound murmured assent from their position, sitting on overstuffed pillows on the floor beneath the Supreme's wooden throne. Only Mess, lying on its side, failed to comment. It was trying not to start smoking.

The visions showed a rather compact but still sprawling metropolis consisting of every known, and, in some cases, unknown kind of architecture. The entire cityscape kept changing as the whims of the sorcerers did.

"There's really no such thing as boundaries around here," explained the Supreme Sorcerer, "especially since the borders keep fluctuating in and out. There's no set proof, but supposedly when things really start getting hot around here, the entire planet will start changing size."

"Great, just great," said Sparx-Slez.

"Then how are things kept under control?" asked Napoleon.

"I'll tell you, you beautiful hunk of feline, you," replied Masterson with a trace of lust, although his wise, aged face negated lechery "respect. All our warlocks and witches are so good by now that a fight becomes fairly ridiculous. We're just a community of creative artisans, still testing our abilities to make life better for ourselves."

"You don't do much traveling then?" asked Harlan.

"What for?" interrupted Sparx.

"No," the Sorcerer Supreme overrode the intense little warlock. "To be perfectly honest, this planet is probably the source of our abilities. Every time someone has tried to transfer themselves outside our atmosphere, they've never returned. And whenever someone has built a spaceship with their own hands and not magic, they find themselves powerless on other planets. Somehow this place amplifies our belief in our ability and makes it real."

"Haven't you made tests?" Mess inquired stridently. "Haven't you tried to discover the source of your abilities?"

In answer, the Sorcerer Supreme moved his wall image into a close-up. There, exposed on almost every street of the city, like road signs, was a small placard whose message remained the same, although the design around it changed. "If You Don't Believe, It Doesn't Exist."

"Our greatest enemy is doubt," said Masterson.

"The second we actually start questioning our powers is the time they run out. It took centuries to develop our intrinsic belief in magic, but it takes only a few seconds to destroy oneself with worry. That's how my father died. Merlin Master, he was called and for his final feat in life, he was attempting to do exactly what you ask: call up the demon or angel who controlled the planet. He didn't realize that the very maneuver signalled a doubt in his own ability. Just as it seemed he would succeed, a baby witch wanted her nursery room bigger. She elongated a wall my father was standing outside of and a second later he was a long smear on her floor."

"Yuccch," said Mess.

"We have our gods," said the Sorcerer Supreme, "and we have our methods. But we have them because they work. We don't question them."

"Now let me get this straight," said Harlan. "With belief and this planet, do you mean I could be a sorcerer too?"

"Probably not," sniffed Sparx.

"It's not as easy as it sounds," said Masterson. "You would have to overcome centuries of preconditioning that there is no such thing as magic. Truly believing in yourself is a dangerous thing on other planets. Not truly believing in yourself is dangerous here. Either way you might wind up with a heart attack if you tried too hard."

"But if everyone has these amazing abilities here," said Napoleon, changing the subject, "what do you do for fun?"

"We have our own lifestyles," said Masterson, "with our own rules and regulations. We don't need enforcers because the minute anyone gets out of line, everyone else can't help but notice it and then there's usually some very fast reprisal. We create our own entertainment and occasionally bring new talent in."

The Sorcerer Supreme and Sparx-Slez suddenly smiled down at Pound, who cleared his throat and rose.

"That's where I come in," he said to Napoleon and Harlan. "Allow me to introduce myself again. My name is Roscoe Pound, director and business manager of the Light Orbit Space Theater, a band of entertainers sanctioned by the Brotherhood of Planets; headquarters, the planet Earth."

As soon as the four of them were alone, Napoleon leaped on Pound's back, Harlan shoved his hand under the man's jaw, and Mess knocked them all over.

Landing in a locked pile, the feline pulled the director's arms behind him, Harlan slid his forearm across Pound's throat and Mess flitted up to keep a lookout.

"We can't afford to take any chances," Harlan tensely apologized, "but we're all wanted as criminals, traitors, and the Destiny Mother knows what else on Earth. What do you know about this?"

Pound gurgled, his arms weakly flailing in Napoleon's grip. Harlan loosened his hold on the man's throat and lower jaw.

"Nothing," Pound managed to gasp before Harlan put the headlock back on him.

"The truth now or I'll rip your vocal cords out," Harlan whispered lightly.

"Really nothing," the man croaked when the pressure lightened up again. "When we . . . you . . . wanted . . . urgh!"

Harlan glanced over the struggling man's shoulder to where the feline lay beneath. "What difference does that make?" he asked her.

"I don't know," she replied angrily.

"What difference does that make?" he asked Pound.

Pound gagged.

"Ease up on him," the feline instructed.

When the director could breath again, he replied, "I won't know for sure until you tell me, but I'd imagine if you are this far out in space that the statute of limitations has run out."

"What does that mean?" Harlan asked Napoleon.

"It means that Earth has stopped looking," she told him. "Not for what we did," Napoleon told Pound above her. "We killed nineteen true humans back in 532 AND."

Even with most of his air supply choked off, Pound managed to start sputtering with laughter. Harlan leaned up in surprise, giving the man oxygen to comment.

"532? Do you know how long ago that is? The Earth you left probably doesn't even exist anymore. According to Muse, there's been revolutions, purges, several complete and total changes. It would be an awfully long time to hold a grudge."

"What do you mean?" asked Napoleon, twisting below the man. "It's only been about five years since we left Earth."

"Traveling at over light speed with an O'Neil drive?" Pound chortled. "Forget it. Muse tells me that the farther you go, the faster you go and the faster you go, the quicker time flies."

"This Muse character seems to be a real information source," spat Harlan.

"You could say she is a conversation piece," said Pound. "Let me up and I'll show her to you and you can ask anything you'd like. She'll know."

Harlan looked at Napoleon again.

"I assure you," Pound assured them, "I mean you no harm. I really think you're both very neat."

The feline let go and Harlan helped the shaken director up.

"Good reflexes," he commented, moving past Mess back into the Supreme Sorcerer's hall, "you two really are very interesting."

The four continued out of the palace as one wall suddenly took on a new shape and the wizened face of Merlin Masterson appeared.

"Really, you three have nothing to worry about," he addressed Napoleon, Harlan and Mess. "Do you think we'd let you land on the planet without some very serious consideration? We'd sooner put your ship back together and send you back to the Mantases." With that, the face on the wall winked out and the group was outside. Sparx-Slez was waiting for them.

"Well, what do you think?" he inquired of Pound. "Can I be in the show?"

"Sparx, I told you already, I've got my actors. If I brought in another now, they'd have my hide. And my hide is very rare."

"But I've shown you what I can do and I'm your official guide anyway. Why can't I be in the show?" The little warlock sounded extremely hurt.

"Sparx, you're a very talented technician," Pound soothed him, this time standing instead of floating in the Coven street. "And you've shown me great dramatic capability and a certain understanding of the form. Tell you what, since this is a type-one planet, I'll be in need of a stage manager. How would you like to handle that?"

"Boy, that would be great!" cried the warlock. "Could I? Great! Are you sure? Wow, great! That would really be. . ." He searched for the word to describe his feeling.

"Great," Pound suggested.

"Yeah," said Sparx-Slez.

"As for now," suggested Pound, "you can accompany us to the edge of the forest and make sure nothing permanent befalls us."

"Hey, great," retorted Sparx. "You want me to transfer you there?"

"This time," recommended Pound, "I think it

would be more dramatic if we walked. Our companions need a little time to grow accustomed to the surroundings and eliminate what worries they have left."

"Right," the little warlock said, flitting ahead of the group, airborn again, as the street fluctuated all around him. Napoleon, Harlan, and Mess huddled together as the road they traveled changed in every way, shape and form.

"Don't worry," said Pound. "Sparx is our guide and he will protect us. Just keep walking naturally and nothing will go wrong."

The trio tried. Harlan had begun to steady his stride when there appeared two rocks directly in front of his feet. He hopped over those to find himself standing on a tree stump sunk deep in a hole that suddenly materialized. He jumped off the stump and around the hole to see a large garbage can rolling down an incline where a second before there was no hill. Instead of walking ahead, he tried to dodge it, felt the can connect with his ankles and fell forward. His arms flew out to catch himself but two arm-sized holes appeared in the ground and a pie materialized right under his face. His arms disappeared into the dirt and he dropped, face first, into a hunk of chocolate cream.

Napoleon laughed uproariously at the sight while Mess took time from worrying to squeal like a squeaky see-saw. Harlan found his grip again and rose to his knees, shaking the remnants of the pie off his front and sighing expansively. Mess went back to considering why none of this was registering on anything but his visual sensors, but the feline just couldn't contain her mirth. Finally her cries of pleasure were cut off when the ground beneath her turned to gelatin. She found herself being somersaulted across the road and landing in a pool of milk. The pool suddenly turned into a river which swept her along its white way until a building before her changed into a gigantic dryer.

Her sodden form was hurled into the house-sized dryer, the circular door closed and immediately all the windows fogged up. Harlan heard her animal-like scream from inside and ran to her aid, but the ground suddenly opened up before him and he fell onto a bed of pies. He pulled himself out of the hole covered in custard in time to see Napoleon come out of the Coven building looking like one five-foot tall, five-foot wide puff-ball. The two stood ten yards from each other and laughed.

"I told you to ignore all this," Pound called from up the undulating street. "If you get caught in everything that's thrown your way, we'll never get to the forest. Now look at me."

The duo turned. Pound stood in the middle of the road with knives, axes, bullets and spears bouncing off him. "Now I could see these things coming right at me, but the minute I duck, they've got me. Just keep walking and do your best to ignore things that come at you directly."

Harlan, Napoleon, and Mess, suddenly completely unchanged, started moving, wide-eyed, up the street.

"Why don't they do anything to Mess?" Napoleon called up to Pound.

Pound replied, "Because it's a machine. It doesn't have a sense of degree or humor. It would be forced to take almost everything literally. Anything Coven did to it would probably cause permanent damage of some kind. They're an inventive, mischievous lot, but not really nasty."

"But Mess is an intelligent machine," called Harlan in a too-loud voice. "His inventor was able to program feeling into it."

Almost immediately hundreds of cream pies appeared from the empty air, all coming together on Mess' floating body. The computer a la mode hung in the air for a minute.

"Thanks," it finally said. "Thanks a lot." Then it spun the filling off itself.

Everyone and everything on that street laughed.

They finally reached the end of the city and began making their way up a small, grassy incline to the edge of the forest. Each had come through his own personal trial by sorcery and passed. Mess had faced an army of little animated rust beings, Napoleon had ignored passing packs of lascivious dog-people, and Harlan had let a wall fall on him.

"That's the ticket," said Sparx, leaving his own retribution behind. As fast as the population laid out problems for their visitors, Sparx-

Slez, the Sorcerer Supreme's official ambassador would protect them and throw back counter spells of his own. The key seemed to be laughter. The more inventive and personal the attack could become, the more the Coveners seemed to enjoy it.

The woods stretched out before them and Napoleon took one long look back at the city they had come from. Though it continued to change color and shape, a uniform style seemed to reign. Almost at all times, there were the spires and waffle-topped sites of castles, palaces, and churches, giving the shifting city a nearly gothic feel. It was a little tub of ever-changing life, like history seen through time-lapse photography.

The feline turned back to the trees as Pound motioned to Sparx, floating about twenty feet above them. The sorcerer nodded and a huge ball of flame leapt up, sending Napoleon rolling back, Harlan to his haunches, and Mess rocketing up to Sparx's level.

"Let's have a little warning on that, Shorty," it said, then looked down. A dark patch of seared earth existed instead of the lush forest. Only about fifty feet of woodland still stood, encircling the scorched area. Mess moved back down to where its human companions were collecting themselves. "What was that all about?" it queried Pound.

"Just watch," he replied, reaching under his tunic. Pound pulled out a small, metal T, the top of which he used as a handle and the bottom of which he pointed toward the sky.

"It's my signal," he explained to Harlan and Napoleon, who were holding each other up.

"Signal for what?" Mess wanted to know.

A searing woosh answered him and all heads raised although Mess didn't have to with his top sensor pointed in that direction anyway. All saw a small gold point appear in the beige sky. It became especially evident when a fast-moving blue cloud moved in front of it and the gold ship, now grown to the size of a dot, pushed through it in a five-pointed manner.

"It's a star!" Napoleon cried.

And indeed it was, a star-shaped spaceship falling down from the heavens. It grew and grew in size until it looked bigger than the burned-out field Sparx had prepared for it, but when it slowed to a landing, it turned out to be a perfect fit. The five-pointed gold star, slightly thicker in the center than it was at its rounded points, landed, filling the burned-out forest completely.

Pound turned to the others. "It didn't have to be this big, but the Earthern Government wanted to be impressive. After all, we're the only touring talent it had." He turned and spoke into the bottom of his T devise. "Beautiful landing, Muse!"

"Great," Sparx concurred.

The entire party moved through the trees to make their way to the starship's entrance.

Pound strode into the mammoth craft first, looking perfectly at ease among its crowded, messy interior. The warlock and the machine moved in next, followed by the other humans on foot. It was like entering a gigantic warehouse with a very creative flair. The artistic aspects seemed to ooze off everything, like honey on toast, and even the messiness seemed different somehow. Harlan and Napoleon were assailed by the stage-bug-bitten feeling almost every human got on his first visit to a theater. For them it was a doubly eerie sensation since neither even knew what a theater was. Both had spent their lives in the theater of accident: reality.

Everywhere lights hung, wires were coiled, steel structures rose to the ceiling, spiral metal staircases lined the walls, emptying out who-knew-where, and huge, colorful drapes hung by nothing across the rest of the walls. Towering canvas sheets were tacked to wooden frames and were stacked on the floor. Props of all kinds were strewn across tables that popped up everywhere. Tools of every kind and description were bursting out of big metal lockers. Garbage, scrapings, wood chips and pieces of metal were strewn everywhere. The entire, cavernous interior defied description. In the hall, there were colors that had never been seen, materials that had never been worn, and materials that would never be used.

"It's just as I hoped it would be," breathed Sparx.

Directly in front of the stunned group were two large doors which stretched from the floor to the ceiling. They were held shut by a small bolt and lock, and they were attached to the wall by larger bolts, two on each side. Pound moved directly over to them, turned and smiled.

"You haven't seen anything yet."

He touched the T to the lock, which sprang open, undid the bolt and pulled. The door on his right swept slowly open without so much as a creak. Pound moved over to the other door and swung that open easily as well, though they dwarfed him. Revealed by the opening was the first theater Harlan, Napoleon, and Mess had ever seen. The stage stretched out before them, made of strips of wood teak. Curtains lounged on either side, made of black velvet. To the sides were wall-sized equipment consoles, outfitted with wheels, buttons, dials, and charts, each section lighted by a hooded illumination ball.

Beyond that were the seats: plush, red seating for the humanoid form. There was an inclined level then a long balcony level taking up the rear half of the theater. On either side were three gradated boxes with eight more seats in each. On both walls were four exit doors, split down the middle, one side automatic and one side manual. In the very back, even above the second level, was a tiny third level consisting of a wall of opaque glass.

"The seats can conform to at least twenty-three alien types," Pound proudly related. "The exit signs automatically change to eighty-eight languages as the creature looks at it, and there are automatic translators of the vocal and visual kind in the chairs. The lighting booth can't be seen into but you can clearly see out of it."

"Great," said Sparx. "That's really great. What does it all mean though?"

"It means, my magical friend, that this is the finest traveling theater in all the universe."

"It's the *only* traveling theater in the entire universe," said an all-pervasive female voice coming from every corner of the theater.

"Who's that?" cried Mess.

"Not who," said Pound, smiling, "but what. That's Muse. My Multi-Unit System for Entertainment. The producer of this space-happy troupe."

"What?" exploded Napoleon, "Not two of them!" Mess started to blink wildly.

"Humanity went forth to inhabit the stars only to find them inhabited already," said Muse as the group retired to the starship's nourishment quarters. "Naturally with the Earthern Government being as all-pervasive as it was, someone immediately decided that Earth would instigate a Brotherhood of Planets with Earth as the founding Father. Unfortunately, as with the stars, something had beaten them to that concept as well."

"A race, which I laughingly call, of higher intelligence," said Pound from a flat machine where he was producing liquid snacks, "had already created a Federation of Worlds which most of the intelligent planets had already joined for their mutual betterment and defense. Quite naturally, not wanting to be left out, Earth put in their application form."

"Not surprisingly," continued Muse, "they were turned down. No truly intelligent planet would have anything to do with the self-destructing, pompous, pretentious. . ."

"That's enough description," said Pound, coming over to where his guests sat with a tray full of refreshments. "Actually, the fact that the Earth's mankind had already nearly destroyed their world several times over made their entry into the Federation unthinkable."

"And they showed no tendency toward learning from their mistakes," said the militant Muse.

"All right, enough already," instructed Pound. "Continue."

"So life continued on Earth, but the government officials never got over the insult and self-humiliation. They passed it down from generation to generation as the scientists created better and better artificials."

"Why haven't I heard this all before?" asked Napoleon. "I was around during this period."

"Then you knew very well that the humans at the time were a very bigoted lot. Any artificial or off-worlder were automatic second citizens," explained Muse.

"Absolutely," said Mess.

"Thank you," said Muse. "Finally, Earth had gained a certain amount of secondary stature, so they again put forth an application to the

Federation. Of course, they should have realized that such a move was prohibitive in itself. No planet should have the gall to apply a second time. If the Federation found one worthy, they would have approached. Earth was again, and finally, rebuked."

"Ah," said Pound, "but we are a clever race."

"And impolite as well," said Muse. "Would you stop interrupting?"

"Sorry, my sweet. You're right, this is your story. Pray continue."

"I shall not deem to thank you," said the female voice. Harlan and Napoleon looked at Mess as one. The robot-computer made his metal arms perform a shrug, then put his handballs under his chin area.

"But Earth was not to be ignored," Muse carried on. "They probably figured that if they couldn't join them, they'd beat them, so they created a planetary organization of their own: the Brotherhood of Planets."

"Of which we are a humble part," Pound interjected, sipping his tan mixture from the clear tube attached to a rectangle. "Sorry," he followed his previous statement with immediately.

"Do you want to tell the story?"

"No, really, I'm sorry."

"You can if you want to."

"No, that's all right. Really."

"You want to tell it, don't you?"

"No, I really want you to tell it. You tell it better than I do. You're more objective. I just wanted to say that one thing."

"Very well, Roscoe. I wll continue, if you're sure."

"I'm sure. Really. Please."

"Now, where was I?"

"At the Brotherhood of Planets," said Mess. "When Earth found out that the higher intelligencia had an organization of their own. . ."

"Thank you," Muse curtly interrupted. "I remember now. Unfortunately, for the third planet from Sol, the Federation had reached far more solar systems and organized so tightly that the Brotherhood had nothing to offer the planets already joined up, so they were left one choice. Enlist the other planets who had been rejected."

"So now every backward, nondescript world that has a race who knows the meaning of the word "me" is under the protection of the Brotherhood and entitled to all the benefits thereof," said Pound.

"You've got to have the last word, don't you, Roscoe?" cried Muse.

"I'm sorry, my sweet, it's just that the whole affair is very close to my heart."

Muse failed to reply.

"I'm really sorry, Muse, I really am. I just wanted to suppliment your telling of it. You had reached a part where you needed a dramatic bridge, so I thought I'd supply one. I didn't mean to steal the spotlight."

"You said I could tell the story," the female voice said in a hurt whisper.

"And you did. You did very well, too."

"How many times do I get to tell that story, Roscoe? This is the first time we've had anyone from Earth in years. When will I get to tell it again?"

"If not that story, then another story, my sweet."

"You're always taking the spotlight away, Roscoe. You never want me to perform."

"That's not true, Muse."

"It's forever 'Muse handle the script,' or 'Muse, take care of the costumes.' You never let me perform."

"Now, you know that's not true. How about the shows in our sixth and eleventh year?"

"Big deal. The voice of Titania, Queen of the Fairies, and the voice of Hamlet's father."

"But Hamlet's father did not have a voice originally. I let you write that part, remember?"

"It was so long ago, I can, just barely. When can I perform again, Roscoe? It's been years."

"Soon."

"That's what you always say. How soon?"

"Very soon."

As the discussion continued in that vein, Mess floated to where Harlan and Napoleon sat drinking their own gray mixtures. The robot leaned over, putting his stomach speaker very close to their heads.

"That machine's crazy," it said.

Napoleon shushed it and interrupted Pound's heated debate with his omnipresent companion.

"Excuse me," she said. "But I'm still not sure

where you and this theater fits in with all this."

Pound turned to her, listened, then spoke to the air. "There. Now you can tell the story without anymore interruptions from me."

"I don't want to anymore."

"Muse, please."

"No!"

"Very well," Pound said, turning back to the feline. "One of the benefits of joining the Brotherhood. . ."

"One of the benefits of joining the Brotherhood," Muse broke in, "was partaking of its cultural services." Pound moved back to his seat and continued to sip his liquid, smiling. "Namely us. The Light Orbit Space Theater. A group of entertainers who move from planet to planet as per our orders on a twenty-year tour of the galaxies, as they become known. Any planet can partake of our services by just letting Earth know. Earth then lets us know in turn by utilizing a communications device that eliminates the time differencial. As soon as a play date comes in, we're signalled by number what planet and when. That way we don't show up at a premiere twenty years late."

"May I?" inquired Roscoe Pound.

"Go ahead," sniffed Muse.

"New orders come in all the time," he said, "pushing us farther and farther into space. We're finishing up our twenty years now with two final performances. However the sad fact is that while we're getting orders from 594

AND, the Earth that exists on the same time plane with us now is at least up to 794 AND, if not more."

"You mean, that the Earth we left is more than 250 years older than we left it?" exploded Harlan.

"Who knows?" Pound replied. "You say you've been gone maybe five years. We've been moving around for almost twenty years. But we're talking to each other in the same ship. Neither of us is less real than the other. But the fact remains that you came from 532 and we came from 594. Why aren't you sixty-two years older than you are?"

Mess' sensors began to flick in rhythm.

"Don't bother," said Muse. "You'll just destroy a circuit. There's insufficient data. There are laws of space travel we haven't yet begun to discover, let alone understand."

"So why do you keep doing it?" Napoleon asked.

"What else is there to do?" Pound replied. "I was a minor government official. And if you knew Earth, then you know minor was really minor. The whole planet was a decreasing spiral of government officials. This assignment gave me a chance to get off planet and out of my miserable position. So now I'm twenty years older and probably much happier than I would have been."

"But twenty years?" said Harlan. "Alone?"

"I beg your pardon?" said Muse.

"Not alone," smiled Pound. "Besides Muse, my sweet here, I have my performers. Artificials created for that very purpose. That's why I'm called Pound of Flesh. I might be the only mother-born human here, but I'm not alone."

"Everyone seems to be missing a very vital bit of information," said Mess, floating across the room to hover beside Pound. "What's a play? What's a script? What's a premiere? Who's Hamlet, Hamlet's Father and Titania? What's to perform?"

"I can answer that!" called out the long silent Sparx. "A play is a dramatic performance of written composition for one or more players of any planetaligy. It's a dramatic exercise or entertainment for an audience. Do you want to know what an audience is?"

"And I can tell you that," said Muse. "An audience is a thankless bunch of unintelligent slugoids, incapable of appreciating a heartfelt presentation of any kind!"

"Now, now, you two," said Pound, waving his arms. "Let's deal a little less emotionally." He waved the small sorcerer to a seat and faced Harlan and Napoleon. "After all the wars and the Great Natural Disaster, there really wasn't very much in the way of literature left. There were plenty of scientific and military texts left because they were underground with the survivors when the worst happened."

"I know about those," said Napoleon. "Larry Baker had to pore over those things all the time."

"Right," Pound acknowledged, without asking who Larry Baker was. "Thankfully, in the years that followed before the radiation of a major war wore off, a certain influential military man had a soft feeling for a certain beautiful female who was dying of a radiation disease. Rather than just relegating her to scientific study, as most of the females were, he treated her with infinite care. Because of her affliction, she had to be cut off from healthy humans so, even though it was just a matter of time before her death, when she became bored, the military official became desperate to find her entertainment.

"Finally he forced himself to brave the dangers outside. When he returned, he was unscathed by radiation and held two purely fictional books under his arms. One was called *Her Lustful Passions* and the other was entitled *The Complete Works of William Shakespeare*."

There Pound paused, causing Sparx to inquire, "What happened then?"

"The disease had gone too far," Pound said sadly. "She was unable to read. So the military man dropped the books, went inside her lead-lined room, made love to her and died with her of the poisoning."

"It's such a beautiful story," Muse sighed. "I've simply got to write a play about it. Roscoe and I will star."

Mess was the one to break the spell again. "I still don't comprehend completely."

"Well, for years, no one knew what to do with these volumes," said Pound, "but when the Brotherhood cropped up, we were desperate for something to perform."

"We finally narrowed it down to those two and *Rare Diseases of the Cow,*" the female computer informed them.

"*Rare Diseases of the Cow?*" Mess repeated.

"It was very dramatic," said Muse.

"We finally discovered Shakespeare, however," said the director.

"But I've always wanted to do something with *Her Lustful Passions,*" sighed Muse. "Maybe even combine it with the cattle diseases."

"So we made up a list," finished Pound, "and the Brotherhood of planets get to chose which one they want and when."

"That's right!" cried Sparx. "And I suggested that they come here. You're just in time to see the galactic premiere of the L.O.S.T. production of *Macbeth,* tonight!"

CHAPTER FIVE

"Tomorrow, tomorrow and tomorrow creeps in this petty pace from day to day; to the last syllable of recorded time. And all our yesterdays have lighted fools the way to dusty death. Out, out brief candle! Life's but a walking shadow, a poor player that struts and frets his hour upon the stage, and then is heard no more. It is a tale told by an idiot; full of sound and fury . . . signifying nothing."

There was a slight pause.

"Signifying nothing!"

There was a long pause.

"I said, signifying nothing!"

"I'm sorry, is that my cue?"

Pound threw down his portoputer in disgust. "It says so, in big blinking green letters, 'Enter messenger,' doesn't it?" he raged.

"Yes, yes, it does."

"And what parts did I assign you?"

"The messenger, the english doctor, the spanish doctor, a porter, an old man, a soldier, several lords, and a murderer."

"Well, can't you keep them straight?"

"Yes, but, it's very hard for me. I was built to tend to the cleaning chores, you know."

Pound leaped up to the stage and gave the tiny rolling robot a kick in the side. "And I doubt whether you could even do that in good order," he shouted. "Get off my stage! Get out of my theater! Go ... go dust my quarters or something."

"Yes, sir," the little thing said sullenly, and rolled away.

"Besides, your speaker needs cleaning," Pound said after it. "Your voice was all scratchy. Robot, clean thyself!"

Pound's Macbeth, a lithe young man with sandy hair, gray eyes, standing about five feet, eight inches ambled over to where the director fumed.

"Well, what now, P.F.?" he inquired lightly.

"I don't know, Sundance, but don't worry! We'll double up the parts or something."

"Oh, no you don't," came a voice from off stage, getting nearer. A second after those words were uttered a young red-headed girl came into view. She was slightly shorter than Sundance, the young man, but with the same lithe, though more shapely, body. Her eyes were blue under light brows and her face held a classic prettiness, one that would stay with her as she grew older. Her hair was a tawny, dark red, almost brown and cut at her

110

shoulders. "We're all playing more than two roles now. I think its ridiculous to have Lady Macbeth also playing Lady Macduff!"

"Flip," Pound pleaded with her, "what can I do? You know we only have a certain amount of machines available for this production. Most of the others are out of service."

"I'll play Lady Macduff," Muse called.

"Out of the question," said Pound.

"Why?" asked Flip, the girl, as she sandwiched the director between herself and the man. "She doesn't necessarily have to be seen on stage. Then I'd be free to do one of the witches and Lady Macbeth."

"What? And have the murder off-stage?"

"Well, that's the way it is in the original script!"

"And that's the reason I rewrote the original script," Pound complained. "What's the good of having all those gory murders without seeing them? On a planet of sorcerers, that's going to make very slow viewing."

"That's all right, that's all right," called Sparx from the darkness of the wings. "With magic going on all the time around here, it's nice to see something straight for a change. We find it exotic."

"No, no, it's still out of the question. A robot can do the witch, but it cannot do Lady Macduff. We need blood, we need an emotional high here."

"What if I splash a little blood from off-stage?" suggested Muse. "It could be a very nice effect."

111

"Yeah," said Flip.

Pound seemed to consider this while Sundance stood back, a quiet smile on his face.

"It's a possibility," Pound muttered. "It's a good possibility." He suddenly moved forward to the edge of the stage. "Hey, Napoleon! Have you ever acted before?"

A small voice retorted from the darkness of the balcony.

"Who, me?"

"Yes, you," called Pound. "Come down here. And bring those two friends of yours."

"I feel ridiculous," said Mess.

"Why?" retorted Muse. "You look adorable."

The robot floated before a wall of armlike hugoes which were attaching colored drapes to the floating machine. All around the small room were piles of clothes of every imaginable color. One each wall, too were six hugoes, with more material draped over them. Between each of these wall-arms were full-length mirrors. It was Muse's costume department.

"I agree," said Napoleon, admiring her robe, made of rich strips of colored cloth which swirled when she moved, exposing enticing slices of her catlike body. "I had no idea a loincloth and beret would look so good on you, Mess."

Harlan took that moment to step out from behind a particularly large pile of material. He was regal in a two piece, shimmering body cast of luminous steel-colored cloth, accentuating his broad, muscular body. Mess' sensors on the back of its head flashed and it squealed in the irritating electronic manner it had. "And I thought I looked ridiculous," it cried.

Harlan grimaced and shook one shiny fist at the computer as Napoleon hopped over, enjoying the delicious feel of the loose garmet across her fur.

"Don't listen to it," she purred. "I think you look great. Nobody will be noticing your voice," she whispered, eyeing him up and down.

"I should hope not," Harlan said. "I'm playing Banquo's ghost." His teeth had been blacked out by a dental fixture so when he spoke, he sounded and looked like a toothless lisper.

"Very good," commented Muse. "That should have the right effect. Let's test the special tactic. When I give the signal, smile."

Napoleon moved away as Harlan faced one wall, glumly waiting.

"All right," said Muse. "Now."

As she spoke, the top of Harlan's head split open and rich red liquid began to course down his face in rivers. As the stage blood reached his upper lip, he smiled, showing a black pit where the mixture disappeared.

"Yuuuuch," said Mess.

"Perfect," said Muse. "That will sure to remind the audience that Banquo was killed by an ax in the head. Very good. Come over here while I get all that stuff off you."

Harlan went over to where a hugo beckoned while Napoleon sidled over to Mess' hovering form.

113

"We had better make sure we know our parts," she recommended. "Have you gotten a portoputer read-out of the play programmed into you yet?"

"Yes," said Mess, internally turning off the head-top sensor under its beret and pulling the script out of its memory bank. "Pretty stolid stuff."

"Oh, well," said the feline, "that's show business."

"What?" said the robot.

"Never mind," she said, "it's a phrase I heard Flip and Sundance use. Now, who are you playing?"

"I play all, what they call, juveniles," reported Mess carefully. "Fleance, Young Seward, Son of Macduff, and one of the witches. Who do you play?"

"I play one of the witches, the Gentlewoman and one of the apparitions. Or is it the third murderer?"

"Better find out," said the machine.

"You're the murderer," called Muse pleasantly.

"Oh, good," said Napoleon checking the portoputer that Pound had given her. It was a paw-sized telescreen with six buttons already computed with her parts of the play. All she had to do was press the appropriate button and her relevant lines would appear on the screen for easy reading. "What do you play, Harlan?"

"Everything," he replied, Muse slipping on a rich ruby robe over his ghost's outfit. "The machines are playing all the lords, gentlemen, officers, soldiers, attendants and messengers,

114

while Sundance and I play everybody with names. Let's see, so far, there's Duncan the King, Banquo, Banquo's Ghost, Macduff, and Seward, I think."

"Better find out," Mess repeated.

"It's all right," said Muse. "This is Shakespeare. Nothing really knows what's going on, anyway."

"Five minutes!" Sparx appeared to say. "Five minutes until technical rehersal!"

The theater was filled to capacity and more. Half sorcerers were sticking out of the aisle walls. Many full-grown warlocks' heads were under the seats. Still other couples came on one body, both their heads laying upon their shoulders. The Sorcerer Supreme, Merlin Masterson, son of Merlin Master, sat in the front row, center seat and, by the looks of him, was ready for a ripping good time. He kept rubbing his hands together and smacking his lips.

Another who could hardly contain its excitement was Muse.

"Isn't this exciting?" its voice bubbled in feminine anticipation. "An opening night, it never fails to give me lapses in my diodes."

Napoleon, dressed in the tattered rags of one of the witches, huddled with Flip and Mess. Pound came by, too intent in his own thoughts to offer conversation, but Sparx flitted by with his best regards.

"Don't worry, everybody, you're going to be great," the little warlock said, lying on his side

115

in the air. "I'll let you know when Pound wants to start."

Harlan, caught up in the excitement, responded to the sorcerer's optimism. "Thank you, Sparx-Slez, and good luck to you, too."

"Luck has nothing to do with it," he replied. "It's this planet and the things we do to keep it working."

Napoleon brought her head up out of her last-minute conference to say, "Sparx, you're incredible. You stuck with this thing the whole way through. You didn't even take a break for a meal. How do you do it?"

"Don't worry," said the warlock. "I'll eat later. With my friends."

"I just hope Pound realizes all the work you've done to make this show work."

"Don't worry," said the supernatural stage manager. "He will."

The sorcerer disappeared, Napoleon went back to her strategy chat and Harlan suddenly frowned, pursing his forehead.

"Come to think of it," he said to no one in particular. "I've never seen anyone on Coven eat."

"It's magic," Muse sultry voice replied. "They probably make up their food when they need it. Like the pies you fell into on the way here." The computer giggled, but Harlan was thinking too hard to join in or relax.

"But you'd think they'd at least conjure up a meal for us. Did they for you, Muse?"

"Not for me, no. But I haven't asked Roscoe. There's so much he doesn't tell me."

"Where is he, Muse. I'll think I'll go ask him."

"Minutes before a premiere? That's absurd!"

"No, I think it's important, somehow."

"Whatever can you be thinking of, Harlan Trigor," gasped the female speaking machine.

"I'm not sure," he said intently, "But I've spent too many years as a soldier not to follow my instincts and for some reason my stomach muscles are clenching and unclenching very quickly."

"Oh." Muse voice laughed in an electronic tinkle. "That's just stage fright. Believe me, once you get on stage, that will all go away. Just follow your soldier instincts and you will do fine."

Sparx appeared above them all.

"We're starting," he stage whispered. "Places."

Harlan saw the girl, Flip, Napoleon and Mess hustle out to the center of the darkened stage. He heard the feline's soft, kittenish laugh as Muse began to work her magic. The audience was cut off from the stage by a large curtain hanging down on rollers. As he watched, the area was bathed in deep blue light and mist began to rise from the floorboards. Skeleton-type trees were lowered in the back and a gigantic painting curled out across the stage's rear wall. It was a beautifully rendered piece of art depicting a swamp. In the corner of the work, by Harlan's feet, was the name of the artist: Muse.

The computer added the finishing touches of boiling pools of thick liquid in two places in the rear and a huge, bubbling pot which came out of a trap door between Flip's and Napoleon's feet. All three "witches" were dressed in tatters with extensive plastic makeup drenched across their faces. Especially in the case of the many-sensored Mess, who floated near the ground, the long cloth tatters gave the impression that it had feet.

Harlan's stomach still tightened and he was sure it wasn't stage fright, since he didn't know enough about acting to be frightened, but before he could do anything about his sudden whim, the curtain rolled up and the play began.

Thunder and lightning crashed even before the curtain completely folded out of sight, giving the audience a vocal thrill. To speed things up, Pound had eliminated the first two scenes, incorporating the information and bloody battle descriptions later. He began with the three witches.

"Where hast thou been, sister?" Flip called, her voice a high-pitched crackle.

Napoleon replied, her own voice turned to a raucous animal-like sound. "Killing swine."

As soon as she spoke, a pig appeared in the cauldron, its head rising out of the bubbling liquid, squealing for all it was worth. It disappeared under the surface as the feline heard a witch in the audience reprimand her mischievous son. Mess, oblivious to the interruption, since it was magic and didn't register completely, said in his regular voice, "Sister, where thou?"

118

"A sailor's wife had chestnuts in her lap," said Flip, but the audience had laughed at Mess' line, drowning her out. She repeated the line and was surprised to find an old lady in a rocking chair appear beside her. But being an artificial created to act, she hid her feelings and began to play toward the apparition.

"And munched and munched and munched," she said. The old lady in the rocking chair stopped rocking and started chewing. "Give me, quoth I," Flip said to the old lady, moving her hands in a waving motion. The old lady gave her the chestnuts. Flip quickly threw them back into her lap and said, " 'Aroint thee, witch!' the rump fed ronyon cries."

"Aroint thee, witch," the old lady in the chair cried.

Flip, knowing that the next lines concerned what her character planned to do with the lady's husband as revenge, turned her head quickly off-stage and signaled Muse with a well-used sign. Immediately after a trap door opened and the old lady disappeared down with a screech.

"Her husband's to Aleppo gone," she said quickly, "master of the ship Tiger, but in a sieve I'll thither sail, and like a rat without a tail, I'll do, I'll do, and I'll do." She accompanied her speech with hand gestures which signified great destruction.

"She's very good," said Mess. "She wasn't this good at rehearsal."

Napoleon turned to the robot quickly and gave it a hard elbow in the torso. "Quiet," she whispered harshly. "I'll give you a wind," she continued quickly to Flip, over the audience's laughter.

"Thou art kind," Flip answered, her voice the consistency of oatmeal.

"And I another," said Mess, indifferently, checking its interior circuitry.

"I myself have all the other," Flip replied, at which point a gigantic gust of audience-inspired wind blew across the stage, taking the tree props and cauldron with it. Napoleon hurriedly grabbed Mess with one paw and Flip's arm with the other. They dropped to their knees on the stage as the blow died out. "Thank the Earth Father the others will be entering soon," Flip whispered, then delivered her speech about what she planned to do to the selfish woman's husband. Naturally, as she spoke, someone in the audience made him appear on stage beside her.

"I will drain him dry as hay," she said as he visably shrank inside himself to the delight of the audience. "Sleep shall neither night or day hang upon his penthouse lid." The man's eyes grew bloodshot and the circles beneath them became as deep and dark as a ceramic mug. "Though his bark cannot be lost, yet it shall be tempest tossed." The man's skin began to shimmy and shake in miniature earthquake spasms. Without getting the signal this time, Muse dropped the creature out of sight.

"A drum, a drum!" Napoleon cried immediately. "Macbethdoth come!"

"That's my line," Mess complained, getting another elbow against his plating as an answer.

Harlan saw Pound come running backstage just as Sundance took his arm and they made their entrance. Upon his appearance fourteen cream pies appeared out of nowhere, catching him square in the face.

"It's going great!" cried Pound.

They had survived until act four—at the moment Harlan was off-stage with the director as the three witches on stage contended with the witches, warlocks and sorcerers in the audience.

"Double, double, toil and trouble," they chanted, Mess acting right along upon threat of disconnection. "Fire burn and cauldron bubble." In terms of that line, they were safe, but everytime they mentioned an ingredient for their cauldron in verse it would appear before them in reality, then drop into the bubbling mixture. Needless to say, the actors were getting a trifle queasy.

"Eye of newt and toe of frog, wool of bat and tongue of dog, adder's fork and blind worm's sting, lizard's leg and howlet's wing, witch's mummy, maw and gulf, of the sea salt shark, root of hemlock digged in the dark, liver of blaspheming Jew, gall of goat and slips of yew. Silvered in the moon's eclipse, nose of Turk and Tartar's lips, fingers of birth-strangled babe, ditch delivered by a drab, make the gruel thick and slab."

On the last few ingredients what the

audience didn't understand, they made up with rather gruesome on stage consequences. Harlan turned from that spectacle, wiping out the gore from his hair. He had just delivered the Banquo ghost scene.

"This is great? We've all nearly been killed several times tonight. Up until now and not counting the intermission, this show has taken four hours to perform!"

"Don't you understand?" Pound said, his face flushed, his eyes glued anxiously to the stage. "They're loving it! They're getting involved. That's what plays are all about. Usually the alien audience sits there or leaves or makes noises. These people are supplementing the script. They're doing our special effects for us!"

"Great," said Harlan, watching Napoleon handle her fellow witches, Macbeth and whatever the audience threw at them. He turned back to the gleeful Pound. "Did you notice the stir during the banquet scene when Banquo's ghost returned?"

"Yes," answered the director. "Really effective effect, I thought. Got a rise out of them."

"It wasn't the effect of my head splitting open," said Harlan. "That I can assure you. They were reacting different to that even before I came on stage."

"So," said Pound, moving over to get a better view of the apparitions Muse was holographically projecting for the witches on stage to show Macbeth his fate.

"So it was different from their other reactions,"

Harlan pressed. "They weren't throwing visions of food up. They were not joining in. They were sitting out there talking to themselves for the first time all night. They were paying absolutely no attention to the play at that point. I think they were even averting their eyes!"

Pound turned for the first time in their conversation and looked straight at Harlan.

"Do you have a point to make, Trigor?"

"Not yet, but I do have a question. Were you fed at any time during your visit by the sorcerers?"

"What difference. . ."

"Answer!" Harlan barked, getting a glance from Napoleon on stage, his command was so sharp.

Pound averted his eyes from Harlan's face, but he did not look to the stage either. He watched the floor then replied, "No, strangely enough, during those long meetings with the Sorcerer Supreme to get details ironed out, there were times I got really hungry too. I think it showed because, well, at least it seemed to me. . ."

"What?" Harlan inquired tightly.

"Would you two keep it down over here?" Sparx suddenly appeared above their heads, hissing into their ears. "You're disturbing the actors."

Pound ducked his head, grimacing, then motioned to Harlan to follow. Together they moved to the back of the backstage area.

"What is it?" Harlan reinquired intently.

"It seemed to be the Sorcerer Supreme was

123

hungry too. Ravenous, in fact. That is, if I'm any judge of character."

"These meetings you had with him," Harlan said, following a different logistics course. "What were they for?"

"On every planet I come down first in a small craft," Pound explained, "to see what kind of society has called for our services. Each planet has their own set of rules, etiquette, languages, and taboos. I try to find out them all before we perform so there's no trouble."

"Trouble?"

"On some planets certain things in Shakespeares plays are unperformable. For instance, some planets who have eliminated crime would not want the murderers identity to remain secret. Others may have something against, oh, let's say women, so we perform with all men. And so on, and so on. Thankfully our acting artificials, Flip and Sundance, as well as the machines, are capable of great versatility. Why. . ."

Harlan cut Pound's dissertation short with a sweep of his hand. "What about this planet, Coven?" he seethed. "What are the taboos on this planet?"

"Well, taboos are tricky. The problem with taboos is that they are taboos. I mean, if they're awful enough to become forbidden, they become fairly unmentionable, too."

"Did you find out anything?"

Before Pound could answer, another voice, strong and strident, interrupted from the direction of the stage.

124

"Thou art too like the spirit of Banquo!" came Sundance's roaring shout.

"By the Destiny Mother!" said Harlan. "That's my cue! Try to think of any clue Masterson or Sparx may have given you," he pleaded with the director. "I'll be right back."

Harlan took two running leaps across the backstage, then slid out before the audience on his knees, stopping just short of Sundance.

"Thy crown does sear my earballs," the stage Macbeth said pointingly, but with relief, and the performance went on. Sundance delivered the rest of his speech about the guilt of murdering kings, the spectres and Harlan vanished through another trap door and the witches danced.

Harlan had to race to Muse's dressing room to change to Macduff for a long scene with Sundance's Malcolm, but Napoleon just had to change back to her leotard after her final scene as the third murderer. The two met up in the costuming area just before Harlan had to go on.

"See if Pound remembered anything." he instructed.

"About what?" she asked after him, but he was already leaping on stage. There were only a few more pages to be done and the show would be over. Napoleon's contribution was already finished and she was flushed with success. She brought the portoputer, hidden away in the palm of her paw, up to her lips and kissed it. Mess, also done with all his roles, slipped over to her side.

"Have you seen Pound?" she asked.

"Not even a congratulations for my performance?" it retorted.

"Congratulations on your performance. Have you seen Pound?"

"Which performance are you referring to?" Mess preened. "There were so many and they were all so good."

"Well," considered Napoleon, putting a claw up to her chin. "How about the scene where I tried to kill you as Banquo's son and you let the knife bounce off your hide? Or how about the scene where you tripped the machine playing the attendant and it felled a whole line of other machines serving as guards? Or how about. . ."

"Yes, that's enough," said Mess cheerily. "Not bad for a first time, eh?"

"Brilliant, truly brilliant," concured Napoleon. "Sharply conceived, beautifully executed, wonderfully realized, Mess. Now, have you seen Pound?"

"No."

"Great," Napoleon threw up her paws. "Want to help look?"

The director had cut out most of the dialogue that wasn't absolutely necessary so the performance could quickly climax with Macbeth and Macduff sword-fighting to the death on stage. It was an exhausting scene, but the artificial and Harlan made quick work of it, learning it prior to performance down to a heartbeat's timing. Napoleon heard the beginnings of that confrontation as she and her computer moved backstage.

"There is nor flying hence nor tarrying here," she heard Sundance cry, "I begin to be weary of the sun and wish the estate of the world were now undone. Ring the alarm bell! Blow, wind! Come, wrack! At least we'll die with armor on our back."

Surprisingly she didn't hear an audience-made wind howl across the stage. She realized that the sorcerers had been strangely unresponsive for the last quarter of the play. It must have been the nearly five hours that proceeded it, she figured, that slowed them down.

"Pound," she called in the rear warehouse-like compartment. "Pound." Mess blinked alongside her, hovering over all the set-making materials. They really weren't needed for this performance and its cooperative and demonstrative audience. "Pound?" she called again.

"He isn't here," said Muse's voice. "He doesn't seem to be anywhere."

"What do you mean?" Napoleon asked the omnipresent personality.

"She's right," said Mess. "My sensors don't pick him up, either."

"You mean he's out of the ship?" the feline inquired, incredulous.

"More likely in his office," said Muse.

"His office?" Mess queried.

"It's sensor-proof," Muse explained. "He goes there when he needs to be alone. I understand. We all need our space."

127

"Where is it?" asked Mess.

"Straight back near the entrance of the ship. See? In the corner of this room."

Napoleon looked carefully and just saw the outline of a door with no operating operatus in the corner of the cavernous area. She began to move purposely toward it, sudden dread crawling up her spine.

"I wouldn't disturb him," Muse said hesitantly.

"No disturbance," said Napoleon, not slowing her stride. "Just one question, that's all."

"He's sure to be out soon," the female computer voice said. "It's almost the end of the show. He's probably working on a farewell speech to deliver. He'll have to come out soon. Just wait a bit."

"No," growled Napoleon, reaching the door. "I think I had better get an answer right now." She pushed on the metal. It didn't open. "How do you open this thing?" she asked of Muse.

"I'm sorry," the computer sadly answered. "I can't open it, Napoleon."

"Can't or won't?" the feline howled, her apprehension rising to the panic point.

"Both . . . it's, it's in my programming. We all need our space."

"Mess," Napoleon instructed, "do *your* magic."

The floating robot moved in and its sensors began flashing in a rhythmic fashion.

"The play is almost over," Muse reported. "The final battle has begun."

"Are the sorcerers contributing?" Napoleon asked tensely.

128

"No, they're just . . . sitting there."

"Mess, hurry!"

"You think this is easy? You want to try it?" the robot said, its head sensors strobing.

"Muse," Napoleon called. "My weapons. Can you get them down here?"

"Why do you need your weapons?"

"Can you get them down!" The feline's voice had become as commanding as Harlan's during his prior talk with the director.

"No," it replied. "I mean yes. I mean, I'll have to send a robot out for them. They're in the prop department, on the other side of the ship."

"Tsk, tsk," said Mess. "Can't manifest yourself, huh?"

"Just get that door open, Mess," Napoleon hissed. "Muse, then get a robot to do it and instruct him to give the weapons to no one but me. Got it? No one but me."

"No one but you, Napoloen. All right."

The feline sped across the room, hopping over piles of junk before she found a metal bar, slightly twisted on one end. She grabbed that part like a handle and ran back to the door.

"I've got it," said Mess.

Napoleon slid over to the side of the door, slipping between it and a table that stretched all the way down to the back of the stage. Across its expanse were all sorts of cutting tools. "I'm ready," she told Mess.

"If nothing's wrong, you're going to look awfully strange," the machine told her.

"I said, I'm ready!"

Mess' every sensor showed red and the compartment door slid open.

The feline swung into the room, brandishing the metal rod, but the sight that assailed her there left even her toughened sensibilities in shock.

Pound was lying on the floor of his tiny office, his shirt torn in tatters off his front and Sparx, the sorcerer, taking mouthfuls out of his flesh.

Blood had already formed a small pool, spotlighting the horrible scene as the surprised sorcerer looked up, the red liquid covering the bottom half of his face, tiny dots dripping off his pointed beard.

Napoleon's mind offered her a quick rationale that it was all play-acting, but a second later she realized the truth. Merlin Masterson's words came rushing back to her. "We have our gods," he had said. "And we have our methods. We have them because they work. We don't question them." Coven was a planet of cannibals. They had discovered a secret of magic but the price was human sacrifice and a diet of only flesh.

Her metal rod was up over her head even as these thoughts flashed through her mind. Sparx-Slez hand was quicker. The steel exploded out of her grip as a fireball appeared between her hands. Howling in pain, she fell back, propelled by the force over ten feet.

Quick as a thought, Mess' righthand ball pushed forward. An electrical charge, burning

130

white, arced out and seemed to caress the little warlock's head. Then he too flew back, smashing into the office wall. The blood that laced the floor was not just Pound's anymore.

Mess shot over to where Napoleon lay groaning, her body spasmically twisting out of the shock. His arms helped her to sit up. The first thing she heard after the buzz left her ears was Muse crying.

"Roscoe," it sobbed. "What has it done to Roscoe?"

"I think he's all right," said Napoleon, shakingly getting to her feet.

"He will be," said Mess with conviction. The robot was better equipeed to make a spot diagnosis than she. "Are you all right?" it asked her with amazingly quiet tenderness.

"Yes, Mess, I'm fine." Although shaken and with her mind racing, she heard her voice also add, "thank you." Then she turned her attention to Muse. "Stop that!" she spat. "He'll be all right if you can stop snivling and get a robot to tend to him."

"But what has that warlock done to him? What has it done?"

"Stop whining about that and start thinking about what this entire *world* of warlocks are going to do to *us!*"

"Oh, no!" the female computer wailed. "The actors are still on stage!"

Harlan moved on stage with the wonderfully gruesome model of Macbeth's head Muse had fashioned earlier.

131

"Hail, King," he cried to Sundance who had died as the leading character only to redress and reenter as Malcolm. He had nearly missed his cue when, for some reason, the female computer's hugoes had not aided him in the change. Flip was fast enough, however, to run over and help. "For so thou art," Harlan continued, his portoputer flashing him the lines from the palm of his hand. "Behold, the usurper's cursed head! The time is free, and I see thee compassed with thy kingdom's pearl. Then speak my salutation in their minds, whose voices I desire aloud with mine; Hail!"

The gathered machines on stage rendered up a magnificently loud "Hail!" then the assembled cast turned to ackowledge the audience's applause.

The audience was beginning to crawl up on stage. Their slithering manner and the expression on their faces immediately spoke to Harlan's heart, mind, and stomach. There was a timeless moment when he just looked at the sea of bodies coursing toward him, but then his sword was out and swinging.

"They're cannibals!" came Muse's clarion cry even as Harlan lopped the first head off. "They're going to kill us all!"

Then all preverbial hell broke loose. Sundance, in his Malcolm garb, pushed Flip back behind him and swung out his own sword. "But we're acting artificials," she wailed. "We don't know how to deal with this!"

"Then act like you're fighting for your lives!"

132

shouted Harlan. "Act very realistically!"

Their two swords swung as one, but only Harlan's met its target. The ex-soldier's blade sank deep in the back of another warlock, but Sundance's weapon was gripped by an inhumanly large and hairy hand. With a tug, the massive limb ripped the sword out of the actor's grasp, and, with a bound, its whole beastly body fell upon the two thespians.

It was the work of the sorcerer's magic, but the hairy, lumpy brown thing was real enough to kill. Its legs were thin and short, but its trunk was massive and rippled with tight muscles. Its arms were bony and long, but its fingers were its killing machine. They were long, ridged, muscular and equipped with huge hooked fingernails that had the consistency of cement. Those were Harlan's new target. As the hands dug down to scoop out the man's innards, Harlan swung his sword like a club, coming in under the monster's arms and sweeping acorss its fingers. Eight of the digits went spinning backstage, followed by black, pumping bile.

The beast reared back, its ugly pointed head screaming. Harlan cut off the screams with another well-placed thrust of his blade. The monster reared back, its legs kicking in its death throes, to fall into the orchestra and crush several more sorcerers. The stage was black and slick with the creature's blood as Harlan spun to face the new horrors.

"Run!" he shouted back to Flip and Sundance.

"Find Nap and do something about this!"

But the feline had already begun her counter-offense. Just as it seemed that the throng of wizardry was going to roll over the one man, Mess' flying form came streaking out of the skrim curtains, raining lightning bolts. Harlan swung in, catching two more sorcerers across the chest as they were thrown back by the machine's sudden onslaught. Even with all their fast efforts, however, one half of the stage was covered by crawling magicians.

"Move backstage," suggested Mess as quietly as it could. "I'll protect you."

Harlan was already moving quickly back, his sword swinging. "Why, Mess, I do believe Baker computed some extra things in your new persona."

"You want to have a long talk about it or do you want to get out of here?" retorted the brazen machine.

Harlan ran, but only a few steps. Suddenly his area of escape was cut off by a wall of hulking sorcerers. He ran to his right: another human wall of inhumans. His left and the seats before him were already filled to overflowing with the choking power of magic madness. Harlan slowly retreated to Mess' side.

The huge throng of sorcerers smiled as one and moved in as one, their faces white fright masks with red eyes and black lines for lips. Their hands were out and their fingers grasped empty air hungrily. They were obsessed, driven by a lust for flesh, uncomprehending, irrational superhumans with a cripple's wants.

"There's nowhere to go. . . ." said Harlan drawing away from Mess slightly. "But up!" With two bounds, he had leaped upon Mess' floating body and the computer immediately shot up.

The mob of magicians surged forward only to crash into one another and fall back like pins. Their starving angry companions, unable to see that Harlan and the robot had escaped into the "fly space" of the theater, continued to push forward, enraged. Their desires only served to trample those first few in line, however.

"There they are!" cried a broken voice. The crowd turned to see Merlin Masterson, still in his front-row seat, pointing a crooked finger at the roof of the theater. They looked and saw the bearded man dangling from the machine, its metal arms wrapped protectively around his form, its sensors bright, unblinking red.

Driven by their unnatural thirsts, the sorcerers began to scale the sides of the building, crawling along balconies, lighting fixtures and the curtain. Some had even reached the halfway point to the ceiling when a group of six white bolts shot out from Mess' handballs which had thrust forward in the blinking of an eye.

Two bolts electrified the lighting framework, sending sorcerers screaming off the metal bars. Two others tore the curtains from their rods, smashing the climbing warlocks to the hard wooden stage. The final two slapped into the balcony, almost instantly igniting the sections into explosive flame. Bunches of the unthinking demons flew out of the two initial fireballs; then the entire second floor was covered with flame.

Above the roar of the holocaust came the same croaking voice. "Patience, my friends!" called Merlin Masterson. "Patience. Quell your hunger until the bloodlust goes away. Calm yourselves until the red, clawing desperation courses out of your bodies. Then use your magic, my brothers. Use your magic to get your meal!"

All the heads turned. All the hands stopped twitching. All eyes turned to Harlan and Mess, high above the theater floor. Even as he watched, Harlan saw the madness begin to seep out of the magicians. In a few seconds he knew the fight was lost. Before he and Mess could get out, their magic would swat them down in time for dinner.

"I can't get them all," said Mess.

"Then let's get as many as we can," said Harlan.

At that moment, the opaque wall of the lighting booth exploded out. Huge hunks of glass spun out and down, sending the transforming sorcerers scattering. From amid the billowing orange and black smoke of the devastation came deadly beams of high-intensity light. For a moment, the cloud cover cleared, and standing in the ruined devastation was

136

Napoleon, both paws slamming the triggers of her beamer and spitter.

"Back here," she screamed to her computer. "Now!"

Her muscles rippling under her rust leotard, Napoleon swept the theater with her guns' slicing beams. Helpless sorcerers were ripped into pieces by her onslaught as Mess brought Harlan to her.

"They can't eat and use their magic at the same time," he gasped as he dropped to her side.

"But it's a very thin line," said Mess. "Given the right state of mind, the minute their mouths stop working, their minds can start."

"Shut up and help," Napoleon hissed through clenched teeth, motioning with her head to the other beamer strapped to her back and another spitter in a holster on her other hip. Harlan undid the fastening on both and started laying down his own cover fire. "Move back," the feline said. "Then run toward backstage."

With Napoleon leading, the trio leaped out the destroyed lighting booth into a rear hall-way. Mess brought up the rear, burning their path with its electrical beams.

"They'll be crawling all over this place in seconds," said Harlan. "What can we do backstage?"

"This is the only ship around," said Napoleon as she ran. "Try to come up with suggestions." She fell to all fours and moved off ahead of him, burning sorcerers as they began streaming in from the exit doors.

The three came to the end of the hall and burst through two doors, falling into Muse's costume department. All her hugoes were swinging back and forth, catching confused sorcerers as they tried to move through. One was strangled to death in one wall arm's metallic grip and several others were bloodied across the floor. Harlan took down the remaining madmen with his spitter, its coiled, tiny, beams of light perforating its targets in seconds.

"Please, please, please," Muse moaned. "Help us. Please."

The feline ran to the remaining door as Harlan slammed the entrance shut and Mess soldered it closed. Napoleon rammed open her exit and discovered it led to one of the backstage's many spiral staircases. When Harlan heard her angry gasp, he rushed over and looked down.

The cavernous rear construction area was completely filled by raging sorcerers. They rolled in waves, rocking against a line of immovable force in the very center of the room. Their voices said their displeasure in rancid, bleating tones, and their eyes actually glowed with the bloodlust they felt. They obsessively moved forward, even at the cost of their brothers in front of them. They trampled, hit, tore and screamed at each other, trying to get at what they considered food.

In the middle of their rabble was a circle of machines: robots, who, up until then had been performing. Even the unrepaired hunks of metal added their weight to the defense, protecting the huddled forms of Pound, Flip and Sundance. Napoleon saw the little cleaning machine trying to smash into one sorcerer's knees, and turning them to red flaked jelly when it succeeded. Harlan saw a disembodied metal arm curl around a sorcerer's ankle, bring him down, then bury itself in his chest.

The rest of the robots simply made an unbreakable band of steel around their human and artificial masters. The wizard's only accomplishment thus far was to crush the first in line, making a second protective ring of dead, broken bodies. Mess, Harlan and Napoleon added their voices to the horrible scene, sweeping the floor with their beams. The swath they cut was wider since their perch was higher. Mess moved down, hitting the ring of fellow robots with his electric bolts, making them deadly even to the touch.

"What are we going to do?" Harlan cried, sickened. "Kill everyone on the planet?"

"If we have to," said Napoleon. "We let up for a second and we're dead. Think about that. Just think about that."

The massacre continued. Then, without warning, the two massive doors connecting the theater with backstage, swung open. Harlan had just enough time to see the clear-eyed Merlin Masterson before his weapons nearly charred his hands. He dropped the beamer and spitter in pain, hearing Napoleon's wrathful howl as her guns turned to liquid. Mess was suddenly hurled back against the wall by a solid sheet of nails, then smashed down by a falling boulder. The computer landed on a row of crazed magicians and rolled, as the gigantic rock disappeared.

Harlan felt two strong, soft arms under his, then turned to see the feline checking his hands. Her proud head then swept in the direction of the open doors. There, Merlin Masterson had raised his arms and the riot ended. The hundreds of sorcerers left alive suddenly became rational again. Their heads turned to face their leader.

The old, wizened master of his planet's arts pointed a bent, shaking finger at the feline. The arm then moved down and a bolt, far brighter and far bigger than any that had been loosed before, tore across the room and ripped the spiral staircase from its moorings. Harlan and Napoleon were thrown across the room by its fall, holding onto the bannister with teeth clenching fear. The top of the structure smashed against the opposite wall, making the steps sing tortuously and the entire length vibrate brutally. Both held on, but their footholds were broken and they swung loose from the metal tubing.

The stairway began to slide down the wall, sparks flying in its path. The sorcerers beneath simply transferred themselves away as the structure crashed onto a table, hurling Harlan and Napoleon across the room. The man hit the floor and rolled until a sorcerer's whim changed the surface to a wet, slick slide and Harlan was directed head first into a pile

140

of wooden planking. Napoleon turned herself over in mid air and landed on a table on all fours until the wood gave way and she was sent spinning from her perch, smashing into one of the metal cutting machines.

It was shaped in such a way that her body was caught by an upright portion while her limbs swung against the long cutting blade. She screamed in pain as the standing blade tore into her leg and arms. Her collision was so hard that her shoulder swung by the metal knife, ripping open a small pouch on her leotard. The four blue stones of Finally Finished dropped out, spinning on the gray drab floor. Napoleon followed them, in a heap.

The Sorcerer Supreme moved forward, his wise, old face lit up by a benign smile. "You are the most precious," he said to the barely conscious form of the feline. "You are the most rare. Your body will have the most revitalizing effect. All we need is a slice of you—a tiny piece of you each—and then we will hunger and long no more. First you shall die. And then we shall feast."

The Sorcerer Supreme, Merlin Masterson, moved back again, lifted one regal finger in Napoleon's collapsed direction, then thought of death. His thought took form before him, shooting out of his finger faster than the eye could follow. His black line moved toward the feline with the straightness of a razor.

Until it passed over one shiny blue stone from the planet Finally's moon. The thought of death was then sucked down into the rock and was swept back in the form of a giant blue wave. It rose out of the floor and descended on Masterson like a curse.

The Sorcerer Supreme only had time to recognize his doom, raise his hands and scream before he was no more.

CHAPTER SIX

Napoleon rolled the four blue stones around in her paw. As the five-pointed gold starship sped through space, they seemed to take the blackness of space and change it into something bright and wonderful—like a beautiful memory taking shape in the real world. Whatever that was.

"So now you have a choice between two world," said Harlan, seated across from her.

"What?" she responded, tearing her eyes away from the rocks that had saved her life.

"I said, now there are two planets who want you as their new leader. Why start working your way into what you might want on another world when you can start at the top of Finally Finished or Coven."

Napoleon let out a small animal growl, took a final look at the stones, then slipped them back into their new pocket, sewn into the shoulder of a new blue leotard. Muse had made it for her specially. "In gratitude," she had said.

"Thank you," said the feline to the planet even now disappearing off the navigation screen in front of them, fitted into the flat of the table they sat at, "but no thanks. I wouldn't mind having mystical powers I suppose, but not at their price. Even if it was their tradition to replace their old Sorcerer Supreme with anyone having greater powers."

"Or the next of kin," Harlan reminded her. "Merlin Masterson's son seemed very grateful and honestly eager to try and change things."

"They're trapped in their structure," said the feline flatly. "It has gotten bigger than all of them. There's no way they're going to be able to control their demons now. In a few years Masterson Jr. will be as hungry and as desperate as the rest."

"Until then, are you going to hold him to his promise?"

"Hmmmm?"

"His promise to grant you any wish in his power and not in yours?"

"Hummmm-ummm."

"That's what I like about you, Nap, your witty repartee."

"Why, Harlan Trigor, you flatterer," Napoleon purred, rising luxuriously from the navigation table. "Unfortunately, we have more immediate things to think about."

"Like?" Harlan asked, watching her curvaceous body move across the floor with more appreciation and enjoyment than he could remember watching anything.

"Like how we're getting to Nest."

The spell was broken.

"Nest?" he sputtered. "You're still going through with that?"

"Now more than ever, Harlan. You seem to be forgetting that since we were on Coven, we were safe, in a manner of speaking. We were safe from the Mantases. But they knew we went down there and this starship is the only thing that's come up so far. What would you think if you were a Mantas?"

"I think I'd be very glad I didn't taste good to sorcerers."

"Be that as it may," Napoleon smirked, "if the Mantases aren't completely sure we're on this ship, you can bet they're very suspicious. And we had better start planning what we're going to do. Where's Mess?"

"Teaching Muse how to manifest herself."

"Pardon?"

"They've moved in together."

"I *beg* your pardon."

"I was going crazy in that robot," said Mess, its voice making Napoleon jump a few feet, her tail straight up. "So I asked Pound if I could share computer quarters for awhile."

"Only temporarily, of course," chipped in Muse. "I don't know what you may be thinking."

"Don't worry about them," Mess told his partner in parts. "They were on the same

145

spaceship alone for more than two years."

"Really?" replied Muse, more or less talking to itself.

"And the Tiger's Eye was smaller than this ship."

"No!"

"Yes."

"I can tell this trip is going to be a lot of fun," deadpanned the feline.

"We'll do what we can to see to it," said Roscoe Pound of-a-little-less-flesh-than-he-used-to-have. "Especially after the nightmare on Coven. We've had a few close calls before, but never anything like that!" Beneath a new gray tunic, Pound now wore a rather elaborate bandage lovingly applied by Muse. "Thank the Earth Father there's only one performance left."

"Thank the Earth Father for nothing," said Flip, making an elaborate entrance in a black and yellow floor length robe, her shapely legs making sudden appearances as she walked. "What are we going to do then?"

"After the affair on Coven," said Sundance, trailing behind her in a simple tunic, boots and pants, looking remarkably like Napoleon's old crony, Larry Baker, "I'd say anything is good except acting for aliens. Sometimes they're too appreciative. Sometimes they want to eat you up."

"But I was made an actor," Flip declared. "It's all I know."

"Twenty years ago, you were created in the Earth labs to perform with the L.O.S.T.," said

146

Pound. "You weren't very good at it then. Over the last two decades, you learned. After Meditar, you'll learn something else."

"Meditar?" asked Napoleon, moving toward the nav-table.

"The next and last item on the L.O.S.T. itinery," said Pound, moving alongside the feline and gingerly sitting down at the table. "It was our last location before I shut down our Earth communications at the twenty-year mark. We created this troupe on a 'first-come, first served' basis." He pointed to a green spot on the light blue board before him. "It's a bit of a trip, but that will just give us more time to prepare the play. The Meditarians have asked to see *The Tempest*."

"*The Tempest?*" Harlan asked. "What's that?"

"It's a beautiful fantasy," said Muse. "You see, there's this man named Prospero. . . ."

"That's me," said Pound.

". . . who lives on this enchanted island with his daughter Miranda. . . ."

"That's me," said Flip.

". . . the fairy sprite, Ariel—that's me—and Caliban, a misshapen monster who is Prospero's slave. . . ."

"That's me," said Mess.

"That's Mess all right," said Harlan.

"Don't interrupt," said Mess. "Anyway, there's this ship wreck where a bunch of people. . . ."

"Mostly me," said Sundance.

". . . go through all kinds of adventures until

Miranda falls in love with one of the new people, Ferdinand. . . ."

"That's *definitely* me," said Sundance.

". . . and things turn out pretty happy for all involved thanks to Prospero's magic. Then he sets his two mystical friends free, and returns to his original home."

"Isn't that nice?" said Muse, giggling. "Sharing circuits can be fun."

"Yes," Mess agreed quietly.

"That will be enough of that, you two," said Harlan. His only reply was an electronic giggle. The actors, director, and Harlan broke up laughing.

"Harlan," Napoleon interrupted, hunched over the nav-table, "look at this."

Harlan swallowed his mirth and smiling crookedly, stood and looked over the feline's shoulder. His smile disappeared completely. Napoleon had matched up the Last in Line's location for Nest with Pound's readings for Meditar. The two lines just narrowly missed converging. If both plots were correct, Nest lied just beyond the final-performance planet.

"Mr. Pound," said Napoleon, her voice as hard as her will, "I've got a small proposition to make. . . ."

The lines of mountainous white rock were piled high. The reflective devices were sending in heat on a full-day basis. Wisps of sun spirits rose off the ground, swirling into clear, nearly imaginary, question marks. The range stretched on forever. The sky, too, baked but with a

148

brown and maroon heat. It swirled, waiting.

"They are coming."

"Are you sure?"

"Others have seen them leave the planet of sorcerers. Others know that their next desnation will lead them to us."

"Then they are coming here?"

"Yessssssss."

"What should I do?"

"Wait and protect."

"What will you do?"

"Others are seeing to it."

"What will you do?"

"The 'Rule' will protect ussssss."

"But she is from Mandarin. A planet you destroyed! She's coming to take revenge."

"The 'Rule' will protect usssss."

The voices paused while they came to understand. The futility of the feline's act was made clear to them. The sky baked, waiting.

"What will happen to her?"

"She will join her ancestorssssssssssss."

"We're flying in blind," said Harlan, disgustedly.

Napoleon laid down her portoputer, pulled her legs up under her and turned to her bearded companion. "How so?" she asked.

"We know nothing more about the Mantases than we did before. We don't know how the new race is going to be born, when they're going to be born, or how we're going to destroy them. This is madness!"

"A madness, if I recall, you were going to

implement by yourself at one point," the feline reminded him.

"That's when I had a ship, a location and freedom," Harlan explained. "Now we're guests on another ship, completely unequipped for fighting, run by a few machines and a few people who are only going along with your nonexistent plan because it *seems* dramatic. What do they know of death?"

"They saw plenty of it on Coven."

"You call that reality? A bunch of raving wizards running over each other? As you recall, they were cuddled together like frightened heaps. What happens when you go off to destroy an entire planet? How do we get in? How do we get out? What, in the name of Destiny do we do?"

Napoleon rose fluidly from her bed and moved over to where Harlan stood by the entrance to her compartment. She put her soft paws on his chest and looked up into his tired eyes.

"I don't know," she said honestly, quietly. "How can I know until I see the planet? You're right, we're going in blind, but what else can I do? This is the only reason I have for existing. I can't go to some other planet and be a religious leader or a tourist attraction. I'm the last of a race destroyed by greed. I must get my people's revenge."

Harlan looked down to her, but he did not touch her. "Your people are dead. To avenge them would mean destroying most of the habitable planets in several solar systems.

They all had a part in Mandarin's final destruction."

"The Mantases killed the survivors," Napoleon said unemotionally as if she were rattling off simple facts. "They leveled the planet."

"So the lion-man said."

"Harlan, please, try to understand. You saved your own planet from the threat. How would you feel if the Mantases had destroyed your home because they couldn't control you? They nearly did."

"I know," Harlan said. "I remember." His arms moved out to hold her then. "Napoleon, do you want to know the real reason I left Destiny to travel with you? I know I said that I had no future life there and that was partly true. The other reason is that . . . is that. . . ."

"You said it was also because I had lost as much as you," Napoleon whispered, trying to make it easy.

"That, and more," he replied. "I came because I felt for you and I didn't understand."

"Understand?"

"Why the Mantases did it," he said with a seething vehemence, shaking her slightly in his grip. "This Universal Rule they keep talking about. What if it? Where does it come from? Is it real or just religious absurdity? Why do they follow it?"

"Does it matter?" Napoleon interjected, not liking the way the conversation had turned.

"Of course it does! We're going to Nest not to face the Mantases, but to face their Universal

151

Rule. What if it is actually tangible? What if it truly exists?"

The feline broke away from her companion, swiftly turning her back on him and returning to her plain bed. "We are going to destroy the Mantas race," she said with conviction.

"I'm sick of killing!" Harlan blurted. "Why cover the wound when we can eradicate the source? We must try to change them, not destroy."

"Would you listen to yourself?" the feline whirled toward him. "How do you change minds? Do you get Mess to whip up a fresh bunch and then switch them in the night? How do you alter belief? Through repetition? Through punishment? How long before the attitude changes back? The choice between social change and total annihilation is an easy one. The latter is much easier and far more effective."

"And would you listen to yourself?" Harlan replied. "You sound as irrational as they do."

Napoleon's face closed shop. Her expression clamped down on its intitial rage, emptied to apathy, then became brutally cunning. "I'm afraid this is logic, Harlan," she spoke, as if to a child. "How do you catagorize mindless hate? How do you define it, generalize it and place it in its proper perspective? Tell me, what did you say when those sorcerers came climbing up on stage after you? The only difference between that moment and my quest is that you had no choice but to fight back or die. I

152

have a choice. I can confront the thing that destroyed my people or I can go away and make believe it isn't important. You tell me, what should I do?"

Harlan Trigor looked her straight in the eye, her own expression tired, wounded, and worn. He moved into her compartment, stopping just in front of her. "I just hope they'll be another way," he said flatly.

"So do I," she replied, her manner soft again. "Do you think I look forward to dying?"

"Nap," he cried.

"You're a good man, Harlan," she said, coiling her arms around him. "You're strong and sensitive and real. You're everything I've ever wanted or hoped for short of whiskers and a tail. I love you, Harlan."

The man tenderly held her to him. "And I, you," he said.

They stood that way for a long time.

"It's hopeless," she finally sighed. "We're in a mindless universe, somewhere in a time stream that doesn't exist on a useless mission with no concept of what is going on."

"It is a tale told by an idiot," Harlan quoted. "Full of sound and fury and signifying nothing."

Her cat face smiled up at him. "That Shakespeare really knew a thing or two."

They stood together in the tiny apartment thinking of all the might have been.

"Excuse me," said Mess.

Harlan sighed. "Yes?"

"I don't mean to interrupt or anything."

"Yes?"

"Muse wouldn't and I really think you might want to know this. . . ."

"Yes?"

"Muse and I talked a long time about whether I should or not. We came to no real decision."

"It's all right, Mess," Napoleon said. "Tell us."

"I think it's important that Muse know it was all right for me to interrupt you."

"We won't know for sure until you give us the information," said Harlan.

"We've sighted Meditar," it reported.

Napoleon whooped and ran out of the room toward the observation bubble in the very center of the starship. Harlan took a sardonic look at his empty arms, then turned his head up to the equally empty air.

"It wasn't important," he said with a wicked grin.

"I told you!" said Muse.

"Harlan! Come on!" Mess cried.

For the first time in days, the man laughed.

The ex-space bullet strode into the oval room consisting of transparent material. On three sides stretched the blackness of space, occasionally interrupted by a clear white speck of a star. In front of him was the collected crew of the L.O.S.T. Starship with Napoleon, and in front of them was a sight that never failed to be breathtaking in its many forms. A new planet, slowly turning before them, flanked by ne planet's sun, blazing in the background with a total fierceness that could intimidate everything.

Pound turned when he heard him enter and beckoned, smiling. Harlan joined the group. Meditar looked to be a white planet, its exterior a gigantic globe of clouds that covered every inch of the surface.

"We've already made communications contact," Pound related. "They know our language and speak it rather quaintly. Muse feels we can hazard a dip into the cover for a closer look before I investigate further. What do you feel?"

Harlan, bathed in bright white light saw that Flip, Sundance and Napoleon's faces held a tentative yes. "Mess?" he called. There was no answer. "Mess?" he repeated louder. Still no reply.

"Mess," Napoleon called.

"Yes, I'm sorry," said the computer quickly. "I thought Trigor might not want to be disturbed."

"Mess," Harlan continued threateningly. "What do your sensors show beneath the cloud cover?"

"His sensors?" Muse sniffed.

"Our sensors," Mess soothed.

"Mess and Muse," Harlan repeated. "What do your mutual sensors show?"

"Well, I said it would be all right to take a peek," Muse said haughtily.

"And I suppose you concur, Mess?"

"It's all the same equipment now," it retorted.

"Nothing to add," said Harlan to the director.

"Fine," Pound said. "Let's adjourn to the control room for the entry." Everyone followed the man out except the feline and her compatriot. Harlan stated out at the raging sun, his ears and skin protected by the transparent material of the room. He looked to the seemingly empty blankness of space and a conviction that was growing in him but he was afraid to admit finally took form.

"You were right," he said to Napoleon, who stood across the room from him, her body glowing gold from the reflected rays of the sun. "We have no choice. Our fates were sealed from the moment we left our home planets. We have entered into the realm of another doom star."

They met in the middle of the room in classic lovers' fashion, immediately and naturally taking each other into their arms.

"Harlan," she said. "I wish I could soften my previous words."

"No," he said. "You were correct. We cannot change anyone but ourselves. They are out there, waiting for us. They will always be out there, unless we destroy them first. It is exactly the same as on Coven. It's now kill or be killed. And then. . ."

"There is no then," said Napoleon. "There is us, and that's all. Remember that, Harlan, in what follows. There can only be us."

"I *hope* I'm not interrupting," said Mess calmly.

156

Harlan's eyes rose to the crown of the clear room, but he did not let go of the feline. "By Destiny," he said. "What ever gave you that idea?"

"It's just that one tries to be decorous. One tries to be considerate. One tries to be kind, charitable, thoughtful, prudent, cautious, tactful, descriminating, prudent, delicate, and perceptive."

"Get to the point," said Muse.

"We're about to sweep over Meditar for a closer look."

Napoleon and Harlan walked, hand in paw, toward the observation room seats.

Falling out of Meditar's sky and zooming over their land surface was like swimming in a whipped-cream sea only to discover a million-faceted diamond beneath. It was thankful that the world did have such a heavy cloud cover because even the small amount of light the came in was reflected over millions of times by the surface.

"It's like the visual counterpart of Finally Finished's Temple of Quiet Ice," Napoleon breathed in wonder while shielding her eyes. The first impression of its composition ran toward one gigantic chipped gem until Pound's voice was heard on the ship's communications system.

"It's a type-two planet," he said.

"What's that?" asked Harlan, helping Napoleon toward the door while shielding his own eyes.

"Type-one is ground, some sort of earthlike mineral substance making up the brunt of the planet," said Muse.

"Type-three is a world consisting entirely of gas," said Mess. "So type-two is. . ."

"Water," blurted Napoleon as she stepped out of the observation area.

"Well," huffed Mess. "Why bother asking me at all?"

The L.O.S.T. ship moved back up into a high-altitude orbit as the crew and their guests collected in the control room. It was a broad, flat area, made up of view screens and several tables where the course could be charted, direction-controlled, and information garnered. All together it looked like a cramped restaurant without a kitchen. Pound, Flip, and Sundance were each seated at a different table. Harlan saw that Sundance was computing the evening's meal, Flip was learning her lines, and Pound was culling what information he could from the computer's sensors.

"I'm going to have to use a bubble," he said to them as Napoleon and the bearded man walked up.

"Like the observation room?" the feline asked.

"No, it's a small O'Neil drive vehicle," said Muse, "that fits only one or two persons. It's totally clear so you can get a good look at the alien life force and the other way around."

"Naturally, it also sends up images of the world that we can study," said Mess.

"The performance is scheduled for tomorrow,"

the director said, so I had better go down immediately. Muse, you start implimenting the type-two procedures."

"Right," it replied, sending out silent messages to her robots, all now fully working.

"I'll go with you," said Harlan.

"Not with all the parts you have to learn, you won't," said Napoleon. "Alonzo, Sebastian, and Stephano? You've too much to do. I'll go with him."

"She's right," Pound agreed. "You remain here and handle the directing chores."

"What? Me?" Harlan stammered.

"There's nothing to it," Pound laughed. "Just let Muse handle the production end and you just keep track of the blocking on my portoputer. Here."

The director showed him the little hand-held view screen, then pushed a button. At the top, the words "Act one, scene one" flashed, then small letters started moving.

"You see," continued Pound, "the robots have their blocking already programmed. That 'H' is you, the 'S' is Sundance, and the. . ."

"Let me guess," said Harlan. "The 'F' is Flip."

"No, I didn't like 'F,' " said Flip. "I had him change it to 'P' for P-h-lip. Phlip." Sure enough, Harlan looked closely at the screen and their was a "P" fluttering around the corners.

"I really don't know," said Harlan.

"Don't worry about that," said Pound. "You'll do fine."

"No, I mean about Napoleon going down to the surface with you."

"I see no harm in the feline coming along. It might even prove fortuitous."

"Just the same, I'd like Mess to join you in one of his manifestations."

"Why?" the computer immediately complained.

"Yes, why?" asked the director.

"Just in case," said Harlan.

"In case of what?" Mess demanded.

"Mess," Harlan said. "Pack your weapons."

"Oh," said the computer. "In case of that."

"Will it be dangerous?" Muse cried.

"Don't worry," said Mess. "I'll be able to handle it."

"Handle what?" broke in Flip.

"Is there some trouble?" called Sundance.

"Take it easy, take it easy, everybody," Pound shouted over the din. "Harlan is right in adding a little extra protection in case of trouble. We wouldn't want a bad problem now, on the eve of our last performance, would we?"

The situation was settled, thankfully, without Harlan voicing the real reason for his concern. It was a shiny, inviting planet of water. No one knew what would be beneath the surface: human, fish, plant, or Mantas.

He watched the clear ball of a vehicle leave the ship. Pound was dressed as he always was, strangely untheatrical for the only play producer to come from Earth. He wore his gray tunic, his blue pants and the tan boots. Napoleon had changed to a multicolored leotard, the swashes of color seeming to swirl around her torso, although they didn't clash with the natural stripes of her fur. Mess was inside a small, rectangular box, sensors along every side with one on the bottom and one on top. The other open area on the bottom housed hovering devices and the grids on top served as a portable communications device, an electric bolt grid and a miniature testing laboratory. A lot of service in its very small package.

From the observation area, it looked as if two people and one machine were falling calmly into a gigantic foam bed. Harlan watched them sink into the foam and remained looking at the place they disappeared for several minutes. A calm misgiving tickled the edges of his mind. Things were seemingly peaceful, but Harlan's every breath caught with forboding. He resisted wishing Napoleon well, even mentally. He didn't even want to admit to himself that each time he said good-bye to her it might be the last time.

He reluctantly left his vantage point and moved through the hallways into the theater. Onstage the robots were unfolding clear, thin costumes. Flip and Sundance were standing nearby, looking into their portoputers for their lines.

"What are those things?" Harlan called.

"These?" Sundance replied, holding up his hands. "You know what these things are. They're portoputers."

"I know I know what they are," said Harlan, motioning to the robots. "What are those?"

"Robots," said Sundance.

"That's funny," said Harlan, sarcastically. "I thought Mess went down to the planet with the others."

"He did," retorted Sundance. "These are the other robots."

"I know that!" Harlan shouted. "What are the things they're unfolding?"

"Oh, those."

"Those."

"Those are our seasuits," Flip answered without looking up from her lines. "We usually use them on type-two planets."

"That way we can perform underwater," Sundance explained. "Slows things down considerably though."

Harlan moved over to where the robots were fiddling with the tight-looking outfits for a better examination. "How do you move in these things?" he asked, kneeling down.

"They've got little grates behind the head, at the waist, and on the feet," said Sundance, "that takes the water and pushes it out in a stream, moving us up or down. There are a few more jets, but smaller, on the wrists and legs, helping us to gesture easily. Two or more hours of Shakespeare underwater can be very tiring."

Harlan nodded, then watched the robots finish their preparetory tasks. For perhaps the millionth time, Harlan longed for his own suit, the space bullet. How easy this task would have become with it. Now all he had to protect the love of his life with was himself, and he wasn't sure that would suffice.

Muse, sensing his worry, tried to cheer him up. "Don't worry," she said. "I'm sure Mess will return in tip-top condition."

All three people on stage looked at her off-stage console in quiet amazement.

"I don't like the looks of this," said Mess.

"You don't like the looks of anything," said Napoleon.

They hovered over the wavy Meditar surface at a height of twenty yards. The measurement wasn't exact because the level of the planet kept dipping. Up close, Meditar was not the shiny liquid ball it appeared to be from the upper atmosphere. It was a gigantic light blue sea filled with spinning squares and dots of flickering yellow.

"It's beautiful," Napoleon breathed, her restless nature subtly quieted by the silent grace of the tiny drifting spots. They seemed to move around each other in an endless swirling ballet, creating grand designs in the water. Mess had established on the way down that it was definitely water in the classic sense.

"Bonafide H_2O," it reported. "Fairly heavy on the 'O'; however, it'll make for good floating."

"Excellent," said Pound. "This will make for a fine *Tempest*. Now all we have to do is meet with the aliens and discover any difficulties that might arise."

"If they have long, sharp teeth and hunger in their eyes," said Mess, "run."

"If the Meditarians don't show up soon,"

163

said Pound. "We may have to run anyway. We can't stay down here indefinitely, you know." He lifted his T device, which also served as a translator and communicator. "What is happening?" he asked of it. "Where are the Meditarians?"

"My sensors correspond with Mess'," Muse replied defensively. "Ask him."

"Mess?" asked Napoleon.

"I've said it before and I'll say it again: according to our findings, they should be in viewing range."

"Is that all you know?" Pound complained. "What are they, invisible? Merpeople, maybe?"

"We can gauge intelligence and react to certain programmed stimuli," said Muse with a chill. "We're only as good as our programmers. If you want shapes, go get yourself a raynar device."

Napoleon tapped Pound's shoulder. "What?" he tensely reacted, spinning around.

"I think they've been here all the time," she told him, pointing down. "Waiting for us."

Pound looked to see a huge clump of yellow-flecked water growing into a fist beneath them. It reared back and just as it was about to slap into the vehicle, the water flattened and the yellow spots spelled out, "HERE WE ARE."

As soon as Pound had seen them and registered his surprise, the column of liquid collapsed and the Meditar surface was relatively level again. Tiny, tinkling laughter was heard from the end of Pound's T.

"Is that you, Muse?" he hesitantly inquired.

Napoleon put a paw on his arm, pointing down again.

"I'm afraid to look," he said, then looked.

"NO," the yellow specks spelled out beneath him.

The laughter grew louder from his T.

"Why don't they speak?" the director asked his companions. Before either could reply, a quaint-sounding voice filled the vehicle's interior.

"It pains us."

"No wonder their language sounded quaint," said Napoleon. "I think they're all 'speaking' at once just to be heard." Below here a bunch of yellow flecks spelled out "TRUE." The feline smiled. The voice had been as precise and delicate as the luminous yellow flecks seemed, drifting their way in their planet.

"This is incredible," said Pound. "They can control the water! What a *Tempest* this will be."

"I think they are the water," guessed Napoleon.

"No," said the voice, millions of tiny sounds combining for a barely audible chorus. "Ship your home. Water ours."

"I stand corrected," said the feline, before turning to Pound. "You're not going to get much applause from this group," she told him.

In answer two large hands formed from the water and slapped together, making a resounding din and basking the side of the vehicle with yellow specks. They each twinkled and vibrated, then fell back to the sea. The T then resounded with a long rustle, the sound of no hands clapping.

For the next ten minutes, the trio in the clear vehicle was regaled by a show of the planet's own. Like a militarily trained team, they created water sculptures of the most intricate detail, their inventions telling a moving story as they went on. By the time they were through, Pound, Napoleon and Mess had a good guess toward the planet's history. A history, not unlike many others in the L.O.S.T.'s odyssey. Here, too, the living creatures were slaves of the planet they existed on.

"Things change here," Napoleon told her companions back on the starship. They had all gathered on the stage, editing and putting the final touches on the physical production of their final performance. "Man had visited this world before, but, foolishly, chose to bathe in the innocent seeming water. He broke down into the yellow pieces that we saw. His ideas, his memories, his feelings and languages all flowed into and through the liquid. Shared consciousnesses of many planets blend down there under the waves."

"You mean," said Flip, "if we let any of the water touch us, we'll change too?"

"The Meditarians seem to think so," said Pound. "There are enough of them now to be heard and they warn other races away when they can. Sometimes its too late."

"So even if our seasuits get a tiny rip, we'll

change into those yellow things?"

"Millions of them," said Napoleon. "Even if a drop hits you."

"Yuuuuuch," said Muse.

"I think you're picking up some bad habits," Pound told it.

"So how are we going to perform?" Sundance asked, obviously not looking forward to the prospect.

Instead of replying, Pound strode over to the stage door, opened it, and shouted in: "Ready when you are, Mess."

Seconds after the two huge doors in the rear swung in and Mess' rectangular manifestation soared out, followed by three floating levels as large as the stage.

"We move these levels over the water's surface and perform in the suits," Pound told his actors. "Muse can control their height from the ship, which will be in a, as fate would have it, light orbit. The planet itself will supply the special effects. They discovered Shakespeare eons ago."

"So we premiere the appropriate time?" Flip asked.

"Yes," Pound answered with relish. "The show will go on!"

Sandwiched between the white of the sky and the light blue of the water were the three levels, floating peacefully above the waves at a height rivalling the O'Neil bubble Pound had first visited in. A larger vehicle floated off to one side, housing the four actors and Mess. Between each level, attaching the stagelike platforms to each other like steps were other opaque vehicles, serving as exits and dressing rooms. In each, Muse had installed a condenser communications system.

"Five minutes," the female computer voiced. "Five minutes until curtain."

The actors were in their seasuits, supplemented with multicolored cloth from the costume department. The suits turned out to be skin-tight except for the helmet that looked like an upside-down beaker without a neck. Communication devices were part of the helmet's material, so no speaker grid blocked the actors' view. Walking was like being wrapped in adhesive tape, however.

"These were basically made for underwater performing," Muse had apologized. "Your air supply is taken from the atmosphere in the same way the oxygen would be sucked from the water by a filter on the back of your neck, so don't worry about your breathing. And don't fret about the jets, either. They only work in water."

Harlan, Napoleon, Sundance and Flip moved anxiously about the large floating dressing room, one wall covered by illumination and reflective paint, the other outfitted with more of Muse's radio controlled hugoes, holding costumes and portoputers.

"I hope this will work," said Flip.

"We've been through worse before," said Sundance.

"Oh, yeah? Where?"

168

"Remember Perald, the gas planet?"

"Oh. Yes."

"The mist kept changing thickness. I couldn't see you half the time. The robots kept pulling us back to the stage. We finished the love scene half a mile away from each other."

Flip laughed girlishly, a freckled hand before her face.

"That was so long ago," she quietly reminisced. "It's almost impossible for me to believe we're about to start our last performance." Suddenly her hands came up, smacking hard against her seasuit's helmet. Sundance hurried over to her shaking figure. She was violently crying. The acting artificial put his encased arms around her. "Oh, Sundance, what are we going to do now?" she wailed.

Napoleon hurried over and kneeled down. "Now, don't worry, you two. It's only your last *scheduled* appearance. After this, why, the L.O.S.T. won't own you anymore."

"Earth will have no ties to you," Harlan said, standing behind the feline, his gloved hands on her shoulders. "It will be like being set free."

"You can explore the planets," Napoleon said. "Start your own company."

"Oh, Napoleon, Harlan," Flip sobbed. "I don't know. I was made with the knowledge that I'd only be useful for two decades. It's like knowing you're going to die." Sundance held her tighter, but his face was haunted also.

"Now listen," Napoleon commanded. "You two are human beings. You were simply

169

developed and raised in a lab. That's the only difference. No one's going to turn you off or take you away at the end of the year. Years have no more meaning. These fears are all in your minds."

"I can't help it," the girl squealed. "Oh, what are we going to do? What are we going to do?"

"Places, everyone," came Muse's voice. "Places."

Like the good trouper she was, Flip's tears almost instantly disappeared and she was getting to her feet. She struggled to find a pleasant expression through her tragedy, however.

"Don't worry," Napoleon told her. "Just give a great performance."

"I have some time yet before my entrance," she replied. "I'll be all right by then."

"Come on, Nap," called Harlan. "We're on first."

She hopped to her companion and the two slid open the water-tight door to their O'Neil driven compartment and looked out. It was a magnificent scene. The opening called for a storm at sea and the Meditarians were up to it. Waves crashed all around them in gloriously chaotic fashion. Muse's illuminations, attached to the sides of the O'Neil compartments added enormously to the effect. With a flash of artificial thunder, the final play of twenty years was officially underway.

Harlan leaped out onto one raised platform. "Boatswain!" he yelled.

Napoleon jumped out behind him. "Here,

170

master!" she called. "What cheer?"

He whirled about, wind tearing at his costume over his seasuit. "Good, speak to the mariners!" he shouted at her. "Fall to it, verily, or we run ourselves aground! Bestir! Bestir!" With that he pushed his way against the howling wind, past her and into the dressing room.

Napoleon moved on, the wind pushing her forward, until she came to the edge of her level. Looking beyond another O'Neil compartment, she saw a group of robots trudge out on the next platform down. "Heigh, my hearts!" she called. "Cheerily, cheerily, my hearts! Take in the topsail! Tend to the master's whistle! Blow till thou burst thy wind, if room enough!"

And the wind did blow, so much that Napoleon wondered whether Muse was completely in charge of that situation. It would be a rude discovery, indeed, to find out the Meditarians controlled more than the sea. With the right timing, they could all be thrown into the alien's clutches.

She turned to find Harlan back on her level in his Alonzo persona, along with Sundance as Antonio and Mess as Gonzolo. They made quick work of the next bit of dialogue, establishing that Alonzo is King and that the boatswain had no intention of being tossed in the drink. Quickly she exited, soon followed by Harlan, who started his rapid change back into the Shipmaster for a new set of lines.

"I have a bad feeling," she gasped to him,

checking her portoputer for her upcoming lines during the scuttling of the ship scene.

"Hold onto it tight," Harlan suggested, completing his change. "Let's talk after our ship sinks."

With that, they both leaped out into the fray again. The first thing they faced were some very storm tossed robots, crying, "All lost! To prayers, to prayers! All lost!"

Muse crashed the lightning and the wind howled as the crew struggled with the shipwreck scene.

"The ship has split!" Napoleon cried. "Oh, farewell my wife and children!"

"We split, we split!" Harlan raged. "Farewell, brother!" He pulled Napoleon to his bosom, falling back toward the dressing room. The robots scattered as Sundance delivered his last lines to Mess.

"Let's all sink with the king," Mess announced, far better in his role since Muse had been coaching it.

"Now would I give a thousand furlongs of sea for an acre of barren ground," Sundance swore. "Long heath, brown furs, anything! The wills above be done!" he cried, shaking a fist to the white skies. "But I would fain die a dry death."

Scant seconds later, the artificial came crashing back into the dressing room. "What an exit," Flip breathed, slipping by him to sneak on stage as Muse brought darkness across the levels. Harlan watched carefully as

Sundance slid the door shut, but the second scene got off without a hitch. Pound was already at center stage in the middle platform as Muse created the atmosphere of a peaceful island.

"If by your art, my dearest father, you have put the wild waters in this roar, allay them," said Flip in her role as Miranda. On cue, the sea instantly diminished. Napoleon sighed a sigh of relief.

"You've got a bad feeling," said Harlan, turning to her.

"It's probably nothing," she admitted, sitting down in front of the reflective wall. Both Harlan and herself were flushed by the excitement of another performance. The joys of acting and the theater had not been lost on them during their many weeks of rehersal after leaving Coven.

"We're sitting on a planet flanking Nest," said Mess, floating by, "where the very substance of the world can deteriorate you and she says it's 'probably nothing.' "

"What is it, Nap?" Harlan pressed.

"It's just that it struck me that we're taking the Meditarians too much at face value, if you can refer to them like that."

"Might be a Mantas transformed down under the waves, eh?" Harlan suggested.

"I never thought of that," said the feline.

"For a girl out to avenge a world," said Sundance, "you are terribly trusting."

"Not girl," she replied. "Female feline. And

173

trust really doesn't enter here. It's safety. There's a lot of effects going on in this play and the O'Neil compartments between levels only block off a small section. One slip in the wrong place and into the drink we go. And there's a lot of wrong places."

"We still have our seasuits," said Sundance.

"Beside the point," said Harlan. "If they rip against the platform sides, we'd have to continue the show without you. There just wasn't enough time to rehearse."

"What could we do?" Sundance continued his defense. "If we performed at all, everything in the water would have seen us too soon."

"That's the point," Napoleon expressed. "Are they seeing us now? Can the Meditarians see? Do they sense us? Do they hear us or just pick up attractive sound waves they translate?"

"What difference does that make?" asked the actor.

"The point is, I repeat, we don't know!"

"And we should," finished Harlan.

"Well, if you'll excuse me," said the actor, "I have to prepare for the next scene. And if you'll pardon my saying so, I think Coven has gotten you two just a little nervous."

"It didn't you?" Mess asked.

"No," said Sundance. "In all twenty years with the L.O.S.T. that was the first real trouble we had. It's an exception, not the norm."

"Mess," came Muse's voice. "Your cue for Caliban is coming up. Napoleon, you too."

The feline began to change into her guise as

Ariel, the spirit, disguised as a water nymph, while Mess shrugged on his rocky, mutated monster exterior with a little help from Harlan.

"For now," he said to the feline. "Just be careful."

"Done," she said, coiling herself by the door. Sundance slid it open and she bounded out, her catlike muscles sending her flying across the stage.

"Fine apparition!" Pound as the character Prospero called from the center platform. "My quaint Ariel, hark in thine ear."

Napoleon made the jump from one level to the next with fine style. She rolled over to Pound, then rose slinkly up, rubbing against his side, putting her cat's ear to his mouth. She feigned listening, while looking out over the waves. She noticed that the entire section under the three connected platforms were clear blue while on all sides, her sightlines were choked with yellow. It seemed that the Meditarians "saw" after all.

"My lord," she told Pound in her best water nymph voice—whatever a water nymph was—"it shall be done!" Then she leaped, rolled, and sprung into another dressing room. A horrid-looking Mess passed her on his way out, electronically croaking.

"Thou poisonous slave," Pound called, "got by the devil himself. Upon thy wicked dam, come forth!"

"As wicked dew as e'er my mother brushed," the flying computer crackled, "with raven's feather from unwholesome fen drop on you both! A southwest blow on ye and blister you all over!"

And thus the play continued. The actors navigated the set well, careful of the edges and expansively performing the magic and comedy. A high point of the proceedings came during the scene where Harlan and Sundance, as the two sodden sailors Trinculo and Stephano, get Caliban drunk. Mess' electronic hiccups were a great favorite of everyones. The watching actors in their dressing rooms couldn't help but laugh and the sound rolled over the waves.

Finally they reached act five and the finale of the work. Prospero was collecting the characters before him for a final confrontation. All the O'Neil compartments were empty and the entire might of the L.O.S.T. was out on the three stages. Harlan, as King Alonzo stood on the third lowest level with Pound and Napoleon as the physical manifestation of Ariel. Sundance and Flip were on the highest level, acting out the roles of the lovers, Miranda and Ferdinand. And all the robots were packed on the center platform, including Mess as the monster Caliban and the quaking little cleaning machine, subbing as Trinculo.

Pound swept himself around, facing the sea on every side, delivering his final speech slowly, to all of Meditar.

"I'll deliver all! And promise you calm seas, auspicious gales and sail so expeditious, that your royal fleet shall be cast far off. Be free and fare thee well!"

As the last word left the proud director's mouth, a tremendous crash filled the sky and before everyone's horrified eyes, the center platform split into a hundred pieces.

CHAPTER SEVEN

Hunks of the stage and pieces of the poor machines flew everywhere, followed by a gray, bitter, fast-moving cloud of arid smoke. The concussion threw the actors to their faces as the robots arced through the air and smashed into the ocean's surface. Napoleon saw the little cleaning machine drop, its wheels spinning and a horrifying wail emiting from its speaker. She watched it hit the water, then slowly sink, curling down like a corkscrew.

The remaining levels began to rock sickeningly as Muse attempted to float them properly without the center mooring. Pound skittered over to the very edge of the stage, his legs slipping over the sides. Napoleon heard the rip as one side of his seasuit tore open from an errant hunk of wood. It was all she could do to keep her claws buried in the platform. He was beyond her reach.

But not Harlan's. His double-jointed limbs smartly snapped into use, his feet becoming ninety degrees to his ankles, propelling him like a crab toward the fallen director. The level swung up, Pound's body with it like a rag doll, then down, Harlan throwing himself forward as the terrified play producer let go. Harlan's strong fingers clamped on Pound's wrist as the man flew into the open air. The stage swung back again, Harlan hauled, and then the two men were rolling across the way.

The level started to spin sideways, bringing the other remaining stage into Napoleon's view. Flip and Sundance had become a crumbled heap in its center, the clouds giving the terrified couple an ethereal glow. Even as the feline watched, the halo disappeared, replaced by a looming shadow that rolled over them all. Out of the clouds beyond the acting artificials came a spaceship. A large triangular spaceship, flat at both ends. A Mantas spaceship.

Napoleon pulled herself up, screaming in the howling desolate ruins. Harlan pulled Pound off the top of him and tore his eyes in the direction of the demolition. His mouth opened, but the shout of wrathful anger was drowned out by the ship openly firing upon the unarmed actors. Before anything could be done, tiny bits of bullets rained down on Flip and Sundance as they vainly tried to move out of the way. The man did a macabre dance before falling, and the girl simply crumpled where she sat.

A moment later the attack stopped. The Mantas ship moved back. Harlan and Napoleon looked at each other in helpless rage. The director struggled to his knees and pointed. The actors were not dead. They were both getting up and wandering about their deteriorating stage like a pair of drunkards. Napoleon narrowed her eyelids and her cat-eyes saw that while they had no obvious wounds, their seasuits hung in tatters around them.

Just as she was realizing the Mantases' plans, they took shape. Another crash split the skies and the second stage disintegrated. At the last moment, Flip and Sundance had found each other, falling into each other's arms as the level swirled off in every direction. Through the gray cloud they dropped, eyes and mouths closed, their faces seemingly at peace. The only scream of pain and loss was Pound's as the two fell into the water. Their bodies seemed to billow out of their skins and seconds later a tight yellow stream poured out of their costumes, swirling in and around each other like lovers. The clothes drifted away from the new, dazzling forms, empty as the dying cries of the robots.

The black steel Manta ship moved in toward the last level.

"Hold on!" came a God-like screech from the empty sky. The three survivors clamped themselves onto the stage as it swept away from the pursuing ship. Muse was back in control. An O'Neil compartment swung alongside, then tumbled onto the platform, thudding its way toward Pound. The stage leveled for a second, the dressing room door slid automati-

cally open and Harlan hurled the director in.
The compartment immediately shot off toward
the sky as the platform raced the Mantas ship
for the Meditar sea.

Harlan painfully crawled to Napoleon, using
his every joint and muscle, his face twisted
into hard lines of determination. She unstuck
her claws from the stage's surface and roughly
pulled him to her, ignoring the brutal pressure
of the wind. They pressed themselves together,
no words spoken, as the platform slashed into
the ocean.

Moments after, the new underwater world
was filled with the Mantas bullet bits. But a
carpet of yellow appeared above the two
seasuited companions and bore them down, out
of range. The sky above crackled with angry
fire, but below was a soft new universe of
dancing colors. The pairs' seasuits automatically began extracting the air from the oxygen-
saturated water and pumped it into their
helmets. The waterjets began working as well,
propelling the feline and the space bullet
deeper into the depths of Meditar.

Harlan felt warm and secure, close to the
way he felt in his original suit, but this new
environment was flushed with light. The
nearby sun, the duo's new doom star, illuminated the liquid, keeping their vision clear.
They dropped into a bottomless pool of beauty,
the yellow specks guiding the way. Napoleon
coiled in the water, initially frightened by her
own feeling of claustrophobia, but when the
sky and the atmosphere disappeared from her

sight completely she was able to relax. Soon, gaining control of the seasuit's jets, she was enjoying the silent experience.

It was not silent for long. Out of the murkiness beyond came a familiar form, its sensors flashing as it propelled itself toward its masters. Mess, in its rectangular manifestation bobbed up before Harlan and Napoleon.

"Some curtain call," it complained through their helmet communicators.

"Mess!" Napoleon cried, overjoyed to see it, but loathe to break the lyrical quiet. "What happened?"

"We sunk," it said simply, keeping pace with their water-propelled drop. "I tried to get a few machines back to the surface, but they weren't very well made, I'm afraid. The water sopped their circuits almost right away. They're drifting now. Somewhere."

"It was a trap!" Harlan raged, interrupting Mess' nearly wistful tale. "The Mantases waited until we were all out in the open, then came in to get us once and for all!"

"They nearly succeeded," Napoleon admitted. "Poor Sundance and Flip."

Suddenly tiny dancing noises began singing into their ears. "No," said the light, sweet voices, the sound of tiny bells tinging the words. "We are not lost. We are happy."

All three did a barrel roll through the liquid. All they saw were the cascading sheets of ocillating yellow specks. "Flip? Sundance?" the feline called. "Is that you?"

The ocean replied: "We are here."

183

"By the Destiny Mother," Harlan breathed, knowing his exclamation wasn't strong enough. "By God," he finally said.

"Are you all right?" Napoleon felt the need to ask. "How does it feel?"

"Beautiful," the reply rolled over them like tickling waves. "Peaceful. We are one."

Napoleon was unable to speak. In the midst of the death and the promise of more to come, there was this sudden respite of beauty and tranquillity. She felt a swift, sudden urge to tear off her own helmet and join the sea's restful ranks. Her feeling passed too soon and her thirst for vengeance, doubled in conviction, returned.

"How can we escape?" she entreated. "Can we get out of here and onto Nest?"

A stronger voice rolled through the waves. "Come." A line of solid yellow formed and lead the three down, ever down. Harlan turned his head to the right and saw a line of machines drifting in a circle. The man motioned to the feline until she too saw the parade of dead robots, floating around an invisible core; the center of the liquid planet of Meditar. There they would orbit until they disintegrated or the world was no more.

The two in seasuits were falling behind. Their jets could not keep up with the yellows lead.

"Mess," Harlan called. "Can you go any faster?"

"Certainly," the machine announced. "I'm also shock-resistant, waterproof, able to withstand pressures of over three hundred . . ."

"Thank you," he said, "but I'm not interested in buying. Could you come back here and tow us?"

Soon the humans were holding onto the blinking red edge of the rectangular computer as it coursed after the yellow piece road. Suddenly the light alien line broke in the middle and coursed out in every direction.

"What is it?" Napoleon beseeched the machine. "Are we there?"

The bells of the Meditarians' voices rang lightly in her ears. "The enemy attacks. They seek you."

"How?" the feline exhorted. "In seasuits?"

Harlan whirled around, twisting and turning, searching the way they had come. "I see nothing swimming," he reported. There was just cyclonic gyrations of yellow.

The voice of the planet spoke again, but for the first time, in passion and agitation.

"The enemy merges!"

Harlan's voice cut in. "Nap! The unbelievable, obsessed monsters! Dozens of them have jumped out of their ships and changed in the water. They're trying to kill us as part of the ocean. The existing beings are fighting them!"

It was a sight the feline would never forget. The sea broke into whirlpools of darting, quivering, undulating cells, turning on each other. They created little cosmos of light and deadly, tortuous designs. As one yellow creature defeated the other, the dying cell split apart, its luminous interior stretching out into

185

a shaking snake, its life force winking out, then *consumed* by the victorious being. Thankfully, even though a veritable platoon of Mantases dropped into the water, the existing creations far outnumbered them in volume as well as experience.

"Come. Please," said the tormented voice of Meditar.

Napoleon, Harlan and Mess followed the yellow arrow down. But where could they go? The feline saw the other side of the planet begin to appear then grow into a surface, a horizon and a white, cloud-filled sky. What would they do when they reached it?

Seemingly as an answer, the yellow line dissipated and the voice took shape again.

"Here. Prepare. They are coming."

The three floated in place, the two humans spinning so their jets didn't push them away. The sea sparkled around them, like a mirror ball, calm and harmonious again. Just before that order was destroyed again, two barely audible voices, calling together to be heard, reached their ears.

"Remember us," said the spirits of the artificials. "We love you."

A silent explosion followed, given sound only by a terrific shock wave, sending the two seasuited humans into the unmovable Mess. "I'm also capable of stationary motion," it said.

"I'll buy it," Harlan gasped as an enormous five-pointed gold star blasted through the world, hurtling toward them for a mid-sea rendezvous.

Muse was crying again, but this time with frenzied ferocity. "Those monstrosities! Those miscreations! Those fiends! Demons, devils, lamia, ogres, harpies, ghouls and hellions! Those malfeasant, malevolent, barbaric murderers! Try to kill Roscoe, will they? Destroy my friends, will they? They'll soon see that the quality of my mercy is nonexistent! They'll soon see what fools these computers be!"

Its hugoes were all flailing away, smashing at the metal it had found in the backstage area. Mess was inside its console, fashioning extra circuits while Muse was preparing the exteriors for newly designed weapons. The L.O.S.T. starship was not going to continue much farther without an offense and defense.

Harlan and Napoleon were stripping off their seasuits, still unscathed while a much-exhausted, much-bruised, but very much alive Roscoe Pound of much-depleted Flesh told his story.

"I suppose they were really just after you. Because as soon as the O'Neil compartment took off, they left us alone. They must have mistaken Flip and Sundance for you initially." Here the tired man paused. "That's what probably saved you. Then Muse and I just took off. She pulled out into a high orbit and we just sort of went hysterical. Just plain crazy for awhile. Then the Meditarians contacted us. A little voice coming through Muse's communications system. They told us where to go and when. It was about that time that Muse got really angry. I don't blame her."

187

The director fell silent, trying to get used to the empty, burned-out theater. "What now?" he pleaded of Napoleon.

"We go on," she said, her furry figure seemingly gigantic on the edge of the nearly dessimated stage. "On to Nest."

CHAPTER EIGHT

Nest was not a planet and it was not a concept. It was three planets and a way of life. Somewhere back in the dark reaches of an unknown history, three fireballs were sent on a collision course. They crashed together in the silent vastness, coiled, turned, cooled and became Nest, the home planet of the Mantas race.

The three half-balls of Nest clung together closer to their system's sun than Meditar, so the side facing the nearest star cooked at an average temperature of 350 degrees Fahrenheit. The rear of the planet, a long valley made by the sides of the two other balls was livable but warm, heated by the sun's reflection off Meditar. The tops of those same balls were hunks of ice-covered white.

Ver few lived on Nest's surface. Small colonies of different creatures made their homes in the far valley and just below the ice mountains, but no Mantases. Their realm was beneath the three balls in row after row of canals, each filled with the mountainous beige lines of the organic incubators, the mother creators of the insectlike race.

It was time. The new wave of Mantases were about to come into existence. A psychic clarion call was sent out to all those who had gone off before. The planet of Nest was calling their representatives back to bear witness to the event—to celebrate, watch over and protect the new representatives of the race. From every settled planet that had enough technology, they came. The Mantases and their breathren creatures. From every planet under the "Rule," pairs of worshippers came.

Gerister was one of the proud representatives of Earth, accompanied by the corpulent figure Broston-Graham, one of the highest ranking in the Earthern Government. It was they who had the responsibility to see that nothing disturbed the event, and it was they who had the conversation concerning the feline's approach to the planet.

"Is she dead?" asked the human.

"There is a 75% certainty of it."

"Did anything see it?"

"We have no method of assurance. Our brothers who took 'the plunge' were unable to communicate in return." The Mantas was the color of steel, one of the three shades the insectlike creatures that denoted their sex or ability. The steel-blue creatures were the females, the black were the males, and the grays were unisexual winged beasts. They stood erect and shared consciousness. Other than that, their thought processes were a mystery to the universe. They were a race unto themselves, following the unwritten dictums of the "Rule."

"Then she may be yet alive," Broston-Graham said.

"What difference would it make?" the Mantas hissed. "Unarmed, unprepared, immediately recognizable, there is a 99.9 percent certainty that she could do nothing."

"What about the other point one percent?" the human whined, knowing full well how ridiculous that sounded.

"There is *always* that point one percent," Gerister declared. "Nothing is ever 100 percent certain. That is why we are here. Instead of worrying, let us make certain that our precautions are complete."

"Very well," the human sighed, going through their defensive tactic for the tenth time. "One of every visiting race has been given a weapon and a psychological image of the feline and her companion. They have been programmed with an immediate destruction sequence if they are even glimpsed. At the same time as their sighting, a psychic alarm will go up, automatically triggered by a post-hypnotic command in which every visitor will be made aware of their presence. Half the group will protect the hatcheries, the others will hunt until everything is certain of the feline's demise."

"And of the ship?" Gerister inquired. "This

lost starship?"

"The same procedure. All Mantas ships begin immediate destruction processes on discovery and all incoming ships are automatically programmed to either do the same or raise an alarm if unarmed."

"So," said the Mantas, "they can't get in, they can't do anything."

"That's what they said on Earth before they escaped. 'They can't get out. They can't do anything.'"

"You worry too much for no good reason," reprimanded the Mantas. "Enjoy the day. Honor the new race."

"And you worry me," said the human. "Mantases live on numbers, logic and rationale. You have no imaginations."

"They are not needed," Gerister hissed simply. "They only serve to hinder our cause and weaken us. We know. We've tried it."

The creature and her human companion moved over to the entrance of their room together. "Enough of this useless consideration," said Gerister. "Let us tour. Let us honor the day." They left the simple silver square and stepped out into a magnificent hallway of rock. The sheer size of the enclosure dwarfed the pair as well as the seeming thousands that moved through the natural caverns deep below the Nest surface.

The centerpiece of the cave, which stretched to beyond eyesight in either direction, was the huge rows of gigantic beige eggs, half-buried in the ground, the larger end pointed up toward the cavern's ceilings which turned colors as if boiling. It looked as though the sky were baking in hues of brown, purple and red. Broston-Graham took a look through the almost unbelievably immense cavern, knowing that there were many others just like it, laughed at himself. There was no way the feline could do anything even if she could get on the planet.

"You see?" said the Mantas. "It is absurd to expect the feline to be capable of anything in the face of all this. Please relax. Worship. The time is almost here."

Broston-Graham relaxed as well as he could and accompanied his fellow creature for a walk through the magnificence of the hatcheries. He thought about his first meeting with the Mantas, on the planet Earth, more than twelve years before. The Mantases, as they had become on many of the worlds they emigrated to, had become invaluable. They showed almost miraculous abilities in the areas of mathematics and logistics. Their long-range solutions to intricate problems always seemed to work, giving the person who had implimented their plans great power and wealth. Their language, too, was infinitely adaptable. It seemed as if the aliens could assimilate themselves into almost any high-technology society.

They had done wonders for Broston-Graham himself, as they had for many other true humans on the planet Earth. It was one of the Mantases model worlds. The people were glad to play by the universal "Rule" in exchange for a wider base of power. The population of mother-borns was small enough to control and the larger group of artificials were genetically made inferior. Their lives and deaths meant nothing. The Earthern Government official looked around and took pride in the number of humans on Nest for the great day.

He moved around with Gerister until he spied a pair of humans he had not seen before, gazing up at the massive egglike structures in awe-struck wonder. The man was more than six feet tall, clean-shaven but with a mop of curly blond hair. He also had a bit of a pot belly. The girl was approximately five feet tall, a bit voluptuous with long brown hair, parted in the middle. They were both elegantly dressed in the fashion of the richer worlds at that moment.

"Hello, brothers," Broston-Graham called.

The pair turned, still awe-struck by the view. Broston laughed and walked over. "Just arrived?" he asked.

"Yes," said the man, his voice light and slightly high in pitch.

"Where do you hail from?" the official further inquired.

"Jackpot," the girl replied, her brown eyes twinkling. "We came with a brother Mantas, a peace container named Penzwinn. Works at a pleasure palace there."

"Ah, yes," said Broston, remembering the establishments where artificials supplied your every wish. "Where is she?"

"He," said the man. "He's off guarding one of the entrances. On the lookout for those Mandarin malcontents. A peace container can kill with a thought, you know."

"Yes, yes, I do," Broston answered. "We have them on Earth, too."

"You come from Earth?" the girl exclaimed, her voice registering awe.

"Why, yes," said the Earthern, flattered. "I'm, in a way, one of the peace containers here."

"Really?" said the man, skeptical. The peace containers had jewels in their foreheads from which their deadly beams were emitted.

"In an official capacity only," Broston said. "I'm responsible for the orientation you went through. Which of you has the weapon?"

"Me," said the man, almost as an apology. He slapped the right side of his long tunic, showing the outline of the hand weapon.

"I hope we do see them," the girl said with vehemence. "A feline pelt would be the rarest, most expensive fur in the universe!"

Broston-Graham laughed. "Yes, yes, it would at that." He liked the girl's spunk. There were so few of them remaining and even less with any kind of independence. "You two work at a pleasure palace too?"

"At?" the girl laughed back. "we work *the* pleasure palace. It's a small one, but we own it. I bought it, he runs it. My name is Fortune-Price."

"I'm Wilk-Perry," said the man, offering his hand. "Both true humans."

Broston took it and pumped it pleasantly, seeing a possible contact in the two. It would be nice to have a new and growing pleasure palace at his beck and call. "I'm Broston-Graham. And this is Gerister, my Mantas companion."

"Good to see you here, brothers," said the alien.

"Gerister," said the official. "Why don't you go ahead with your work while I talk to these two charming people?"

"No harm," the Mantas decided, knowing full well the influential human was going to try and make a deal. "No harm, I will see you soon by the mother creator, I hope." The tone of the alien's hissing voice left little doubt in the trio's mind that Gerister was issuing an order.

"Absolutely," said Broston-Graham.

"Of course," said the other two.

Gerister moved away, joining another trio of aliens as they wandered about.

"Come," said the human official. "Shall we step inside my office for a moment?"

As soon as he had moved back into the small silver box by the corner of the cavern, he felt a rock-hard hand clamp around the back of his neck and the barrel of a gun jam under his chin. Both were extremely effective in silencing him. He desperately hoped that his two companions would do something about the attack, but when he was spun around he saw that his two companions were doing the attacking!

The man held his inexorable grip, while the

girl began tearing at her own skull. With a small sucking noise, her hair came off in her hands, exposing a bald head and two catlike ears. Broston-Graham's eyes widened in shock and fear. The girl's own eyes popped out immediately after, the two contact lenses exposing green cat eyes.

"Thank the Earth Father," she whispered. "I couldn't take those much longer."

The Earthern Government man couldn't believe his eyes and ears. The feline had completely shorn herself of fur and added false appendages to make up for her lack of human face! She pulled her floor-length garment off, exposing her lithe frame in a leotard with two weapons strapped under large breast shapers. Her skin was slightly red from the shaving, but it was clear and amazingly womanlike. She also kicked off the boots that added five inches to her height. Her final action, while keeping most of her facial makeup on, was to pull out a spitter and stick it in Broston-Graham's mouth.

"I'm betting," she hissed, "that Earth people haven't changed that much since I left. I'm betting you're more eager to save your own life than raise an alarm. You know my reputation. I'd kill humans rather than eat. What is it going to be, Broston-Graham? Survival? Or a martyr's funeral?"

Broston-Graham walked with Fortune-Price and Wilk-Perry toward the mother creator. Their clothes flowed through the heated rock hallways, brushing against each other. Their proximity effectively cut off sight lines of the Mantas weapon held in Napoleon's gloved paw. All her disguise was back on again, supplementing the almost entirely false face Muse worked up for her. It had taken six hours to apply and was uncomfortable as all get-out, but the effect was worth it. The feline seemed to be a complete human being.

Harlan's guise was less complicated, but just as effective, boots giving him extra height, makeup to make him paler, plus a shave and a curly blond wig. Blue contact lenses and padding completed the effect, turning his normally dark eyes light and giving his tight muscles some fat. He held a short, wicked metal blade Muse had fashioned out of a prop against the official's chubby side.

"There's nothing you can do," Broston-Graham whispered out of the corner of his mouth.

"Just lead us to this mother creator," Napoleon said quietly but pleasantly, as if they were great friends. "And act naturally."

"I'm not very good at acting," Broston complained.

"If we can do it," said Harlan, "anybody can."

"But I tell you it's no good," Broston continued, smiling. "There's too many Mantases on the planet. Once you do anything, they'll all know about it, and every living thing on this world will hunt you down. Tell you what. Get off the way you got on. Escape. I won't tell."

"We came here because we had to," said Napoleon.

"It's absurd," the official whispered. "There's too many hatcheries on the planet. Each run by a separate mother creator. You can never get them all. Run, run while you still can."

"This looks like it," Harlan said. "Shut up."

The trio had come to the rear of a huge throng at the end of a line of large beige mountains. Atop a natural pulpit stood Gerister, a steel blue thing against a balcony carved out of solid rock. A stone stairway led up to the summit on its left side and when the Mantas spied Broston-Graham, she motioned him forward.

"Remember," Napoleon told him affably as he went. "I'm an incredible shot. A word and you'll be dead before we will. Remember."

The human official rose to join his alien companion on the pulpit, a very exposed spot. Thankfully, he was not sweating but his eyes told Harlan he was considering the odds for a hundred alternatives.

"It won't last long," he whispered to the disguised feline. "Whatever we do, we'll have to do it soon and in one fell swoop."

The two moved until all the gathered races had crowded before the steel blue Mantas. Napoleon and Harlan stood in the rear of the crowd, their sights still clear on Broston-Graham. Both knew that as soon as he was out of their view, an alarm would be raised and they were as good as dead. The throng numbered a little more than six thousand when Gerister raised her mandibles.

"The Mantas race has been adding to the universe's might for centuries," the creature hissed, her voice echoing naturally along the cave walls. "We lust for order. A common order, unfettered by race or boundaries. Where none exists, we create it."

"They know we're here," Napoleon suddenly snarled in Harlan's ear, her arms shrinking into her long robes, grabbing at her other weapons.

"Stop," Harlan commanded. "What do you mean? Explain."

"This is the same speech another Mantas gave to me on Destiny," the feline uttered. "Almost word for word."

"Of course," Harlan quickly soothed, his own nerves jangling. "They share consciousnesses. They all serve the "Rule." They all know the propaganda."

Several mob members turned angrily toward the two, their faces demanding silence as Gerister continued.

"We are seeded throughout the galaxies by the mother creator," the Mantas declared, turning slightly and pointing to a wall of bubbling rock. "The race travels through space, pinpointing worlds outside the universal "Rule." We strive to unite each under the "Rule," the only true rule, no matter how many eons it takes!"

At that, the throng broke into wild cheers, praising their religion to the baking ceiling.

"Where there is one Mantas there is all

Mantases!" Gerister screamed. The scream was echoed by the frenzied cries of her audience. All arms were up, all eyes were alight with the inner fire. Once again Napoleon and Harlan had come up against the evil conquerers. Ones so fanatical that they were willing to commit mass suicide to achieve their ends. The realization struck Napoleon with a hammer's blow.

"Harlan," she hissed in his ear. "How are the Mantases seeded?"

"The mother creator does it. She just said so."

"But *how*? Look at the ceiling. Look at the mountains' shapes. What does it suggest to you?"

Harlan glanced at the boiling brown cave tops, swirling in individual circles. He looked to the egglike mounds, each seeming to point at a separate ceiling swirl. He looked back at the line of beige hills, all neat, all in organized rows, like line upon line of. . .

"Missiles," he breathed, aghast. "Rockets. Weapons. Lasers. By God."

"They're blasted out," said Napoleon. "And these representatives have been gathered to die in the glory of the new race. We're sacrifices to make sure all goes well!"

"That's madness," Harlan told her.

"Have you been listening to her speak?" The feline motioned toward the passion-filled Gerister. "What would *you* call this cultish drivel?"

Harlan stared off toward the Mantas who

was still foaming rhetoric. "Broston-Graham. He doesn't know?"

"How could he? How could any of them? They're blinded by the security and power. The Mantases are complegely in control."

Harlan pulled the forefinger of his up to his mouth. The micro-circuit communications device Mess had installed there worked perfectly. "Get ready," he told it. Thankfully, since he was in the rear of the crowd, no one took notice of this erratic behavior. "Let's get out of here."

The two began to move slowly away from the mass.

"What about Broston?" Napoleon whispered.

"Hopefully he'll think that we've come to our senses and are trying to escape. Given his ego, maybe he won't announce our presence for at least a minute."

The two moved behind a turn in the cavern, cutting them off from most of the hatching festivities. Without making sure, the two both began to run, their hearts beating like mad.

"How soon do you think the hatching will start?" Harlan asked her, not slowing his pace.

"The Mantases can't give anything time to realize what is going to happen," puffed Napoleon, pulling off her wig, and kicking off her boots as they raced. "I'd say very soon now." She pulled open her robe, throwing it behind her and pulled off a holstered spitter. "Here," she said, throwing it to Harlan. He caught it with one hand and brought the fingernail communicator up with his other.

"Things are going to blow any second down here," he told a listening Mess. "Come in under the subsequent fire." He then dropped his hand and strapped on the gun, sticking the Mantas hand weapon in his teeth.

Napoleon dropped to all fours, and her tail, which until then she had coiled around her waist like a belt, slashed back and forth. Harlan's Destiny-trained muscles responded to her new speed and the two raced through the hallway of imminent death. Just as the cave's entrance appeared before them, they heard a vastly echoed human scream coming from the mother-creator location.

"Broston must have discovered his fate," Napoleon shouted behind her. "Get ready."

Harlan pulled the Mantas weapon down as he ran full speed toward the entrance. Flanking the circular opening were six rifle-toting Mantases, two of each kind. "Drop the winged ones first," Harlan shouted. "They're the most dangerous to us."

At the sound of his voice, the twitching aliens turned toward them. They had to shake off their own religious fervor just prior to the hatching, which gave the humans the edge. Napoleon dropped to her stomach, Harlan dropped to his knees and they both slid and fired. The feline's hand beamer sliced a male and a flier in half while Harlan's Mantas weapon was a spinner, shooting tiny, twirling projectiles which bore into the target. In this case, it was the upper torso of the second flier.

Harlan immediately drew his hand beamer from the holster and all three weapons joined in. Before the remaining Mantases were able to even aim, they were turned into dark piles of nasty-smelling waste. A roar from the victors' backs told them that the hatching process had started and the worshippers were desperately trying to escape. Dark, boiling hunks of the ceiling began to drop all around them.

"Run!" Harlan screamed. "The entire cavern will be cut off in a second!"

The ground shook and a large piece of the ceiling splashed hotly down between the feline and the space bullet. Napoleon spent no time galloping on all fours out of the cave. As she fell and rolled, seemingly half the hillside fell before the rock entrance. She rolled over, sat up, looked for Harlan, then immediately began bathing the fallen earth with her beamer.

A hole suddenly appeared in the smoking mass and the man leaped out like a professional diver, his incredibly powerful muscles propelling him to an incredible height. He dropped like a cat and rolled, his body taking the brunt with style.

"I was hoping you'd do that," he told the feline.

"You wig is on fire," she replied. Harlan pulled off the blond, flaming mop and threw it away before burning his fingers could burn any more. "I'm glad we shaved," Napoleon finished, "or else we'd be far worse off than we are now."

"What could be worse?" Harlan asked, crouching beside her.

In answer, the planet exploded. It was like being caught in the midst of heavy artillery with a pop gun. First the ground began to shake, then huge, gaping holes just caved in. Then boiling mud and burning hot rocks were thrown up like gushers. Harlan and the feline immediately opened their beamers up to the widest aperture and bathed the sky above their heads with a high-intensity orange umbrella. That didn't prevent new rivers of molten mud to start cooking their shoes and passing fields of hurtling rocks to bombard them, though. It merely prevented huge waves of dirt and boulders from crushing them.

The bruising rocks pummeled them into one another, their beamer hands waving jerkily from the sudden pain. As the last of the schrapnel fell, the two dropped to the ground, each bleeding from the face and body. It had been like being mugged by an invisible army.

Then the shells began to take off.

Millions of dark bullets began to spew out of the entire landscape. They streamed out so fast that there was barely any sound but a slight sweeping noise. And they came from everywhere. They were six-feet long tubes, rounded off and closed at each end. They followed one another by inches so they appeared to be round piping reaching up to the sky. The entire planet's surface, facing away from the sun, was obliterated by their disgusting streams. They were like millions of tentacle-sized follicles growing out of a head through the magic of time-lapse photography.

They stretched out into space and began to dissipate, moving off in all directions toward their previously established destinations. Harlan and Napoleon sat groaning, safe in the eye of a hurricane as the doom they sought to prevent blasted off all around them.

Napoleon crawled into Harlan's lap, big clear tears pouring out of her green eyes. She hugged him to her and moaned. "We've lost. I've failed." She rubbed herself against his torso, hearing a sudden crunching. She moved again and the crunching returned. It was coming from her shoulder. "The stones!" she cried. "The Last in Line's stones."

The feline sat up among the blasting shells and emptied her leotard's shoulder pocket into her hand. But instead of the four small stones, out came sparkling blue dust. Napoleon realized that the rain of rocks that had assailed them must have crushed the Finally stones as well. Her bitter tears fell into her hand, splashing onto the blue ground, a fitting symbol of her destroyed dreams.

The blue dust began to bubble.

In shock, Napoleon fell back, the dust cascading down through the air and falling between her crossed legs. The blue remnants disappeared into Nest's surface. Immediately after, the ground began to shake anew. Harlan pulled Napoleon to her feet and, holding her paw, ran. He dodged between the spewing Mantas shells, pushing his battered legs for all they were worth.

"Stay in one place!" cried Mess' voice from his fingertip. "We've almost maneuvered between these geysers, but we can't get you pinpointed! Just stay in one spot for a minute!"

Harlan held the tearful Napoleon with one arm and brought the communicator up to his mouth. "Hurry, Mess. This entire area will probably collapse any time."

"I show no sign of geological weakness," Muse butted in.

"Call it an educated guess," said Harlan. "Just get us out of here!"

Seconds later a shadow descended on the pair as the ground began to roll, like the surface of Finally Finished. Harlan looked up to see an O'Neil-driven compartment, sent over from the frozen wastes of Nest, coming in for a landing beside them. Just as it set down, the waves of Mantas eggs began to stop. Then it continued at its regular pace. Then it stopped again. Suddenly the eggs were blasting off in all directions, waving crazily in wide arcs.

Harlan pulled himself and Napoleon into the O'Neil compartment. Just as the door was sliding shut he saw that incomplete Mantases, still surrounded by birth fluid, had begun spitting out of the holes *without* shells. The liquid dropped off them and their limbs spread out slowly before they fell to the ground again with a sickening splat. Soon the entire departure and hatching deteriorated. Hunks of Mantas hide spewed out of the holes like living diarrhea, crashing into each other and the compartment.

The O'Neil drive went on full tilt thanks to Mess, and the small flying room blasted out from under the remnants of the new Mantas civilization. Harlan and Napoleon hugged each other with brute fear and strength, lying in a boiled pile on the dressing room floor, until the compartment door opened again and Mess' hovering sensors were flashing in at them.

"Better come on out," it said with undisguised glee. "You aren't going to believe this."

The pair raced their computer to the L.O.S.T. starship's observation area, where Pound stood, hopping up and down with maniacal glee.

"Look!" he cried, pointing to outer space beyond. "Look!"

The sky was filled with ships. And they weren't Mantas ships. They were incredible intricate spaceships of so many designs, Harlan couldn't recognize even one. The Mantas ships and the traveling shells they were out to protect, were being unmercifully destroyed. Napoleon could barely keep up with the number of little, silent explosions as they appeared to her for minute after minute.

The Mantases were being, incredibly and without exception, routed by an unknown fleet of incredibly powerful ships.

"What is happening?" Harlan cried. "Where

are all these ships from? Coven? Meditar? Destiny?"

"Well," said a new male voice, full of grace and humor. "Yes and no."

The space bullet and the feline spun around to the speaker. Standing in the observation room entrance, twenty years older, but just as fit as before, was Larry Baker.

CHAPTER NINE

The massacre was over. These things, once started, usually ended very quickly, Larry assured his friends. All the Mantas hatchings had been destroyed en route. All the existing Mantas spaceships had been blasted, and the planet itself was being torn to shreds by a cataclysm of natural disasters. The universal "Rule" had ended without the destroyers knowing anything more about it than when it first appeared.

Napoleon, Harlan and Mess sat in the shining control room of Larry's new ship, lovingly christened the Black Hole III. "II had been badly battered by a Destiny range war sixteen years back," Baker had informed them. "The Black Hole is a Federation ship now. About ten years ago the Federation approached Destiny's Queen and offered their services and membership. We naturally agreed. It was a great honor for the Garden Planet, so soon after our Mantas purge."

"So you were all trailing the Mantases until this new hatching occurred?" Napoleon asked.

"Some were," Larry admitted, putting a hand through the silver hair at his temples. He wore a uniform of a high-ranking Federation member, but over his left breast was the brown and green Destiny patch. "I was following you."

"Me!" the feline exclaimed, rubbing at her bandaged bruises. "Why?"

"Mandarin was one of the founding members of the Federation," he replied, looking at both his old copilot and Harlan, "back in a time stream before the organization was powerful and far-reaching. By the time the Federation could mount a counter-offensive against the purgers of the planet, it was too late. Naturally, as the last remaining member of the Mandarin race, you deserved the protection of the Federation. That led me, as a new member of the group, to Finally Finished."

"You met the Last in Line?" Harlan inquired.

"I was there at his burial and I heard about your visit. I also discovered that the four Mandarin Gems were missing."

"Four *Mandarin* gems?" the feline echoed.

"That's right," Larry explained. "They were taken from their sacred place by the Last in Line to the moon of Finally where he thought they would be safe. These stones had the

212

capability of magnifying and transforming emotions into a plane of reality. That's as near as I can get to understand their properties."

"So they were able to cut into the Mantas 'assembly line' even as dust," Harlan surmised.

"Probably," agreed Larry. "Though with the power of the Federation's defenses, it is still questionable what destroyed the planet Nest."

"How did you get here?" Napoleon wanted to know.

"And why are you so *old?*" Mess asked subtly.

Larry laughed. "Blame it on the as yet unknown time streams," he said. "As far as I know, my life has been going along very well by seasons. And although it may take several months to return to Destiny, the planet would be the same as I left it. I couldn't say the same if you were to try it."

"What if we went together?" suggested Harlan.

"I don't know," Larry replied. "Want to try it?"

"No, thank you," said Mess. "I wouldn't want to rust away before my very sensors." The trio of humans laughed. "Well, it's as near as I can come to understanding this space-travel madness," the computer complained.

"I can't explain it either," Larry continued after their mirth had diminished. "No one else has been able to, just the same. Those who might have experimented successfully never returned to talk about it. Not to the Federation, at least. So ignoring whatever laws govern time, I joined my fleet and we trailed a group of Mantas representatives back to the home planet in time for the hatching. Then it was simply a case of finishing the job we all started on Destiny twenty years ago."

"How is my sister?" asked Harlan, gently caressed by her memory. "Your wife?"

"More precious and beautiful by the day," Larry said. "Do you know I think she is even better looking at forty than she was at twenty?"

"She had better be," Harlan answered, "to your eyes."

"She is," Baker said honestly. "The only reason I'm here now was that I had a personal stake in this mission." His gray eyes focused on Napoleon, her fur already beginning to grow back, sprouting like peach fuzz all over her body. "I'm glad I could see you again, Nap."

"And I you," she said, her eyes misting.

"Here comes the romantic stuff," complained Mess.

"Come on, you titanic tribute to terrible timing," said Harlan, tapping the bottom of Mess' floating form with his fist. "Let's take a look around, then head back to the L.O.S.T. ship."

Mess went with the tall figure, electronically whining, "But he's so *old!*"

Harlan stopped by the exit out of Larry's ship. "It was good seeing you, Larry. Please love my sister."

"For both of us," Baker replied. And then Harlan was gone.

The two people just looked at each other awhile. It was as if they were afraid to let their two worlds touch. Napoleon spoke first.

"You're not really here, are you?" she asked, more of herself than her old partner and friend. "You're part of a future I know nothing of, and a past I can barely remember. Has it only been two years?"

"Twenty," said Larry sadly. They remained silent for another period, both looking everywhere but at each other. "I'm very happy," Larry finally said. "My life has been full."

Silence reigned again.

"There's nothing to say, Larry," Napoleon told him. "We said it all when we parted. Let this be a passing dream. A wonderful moment when we see each other again and know that everything is all right."

"Are you all right?" he asked, quietly ashamed.

"I will be," she said with defiance.

Larry Baker's face slowly drooped down into an expression of despair and shared pain. His next words came in a distinct but rushed whisper.

"You cannot mate with him," he said. "You cannot mate with anything but your own kind. I know. The Federation informed me. Your love will kill you."

"It sounds peaceful."

"It's painful. Months of wracking torture." Baker cut his words off, his face flushing with shame. "You had to know," he told himself. "I had to tell you."

"I knew," Napoleon said simply.

Baker looked up into her eyes. "Is there anything for you? Anywhere?"

Napoleon looked back, her face composed. "There's Harlan. Still. And a promise. A promise from a planet called Coven."

The two old friends sat facing each other in silence.

"I love you," the feline finally said.

"I love you," he replied. There words carried no volume or tone. They were spoken flatly but still the words, across miles and light years and time, had weight.

"I'll go," said Larry.

Without another word the two friends parted forever.

Napoleon found Harlan alone in the L.O.S.T. observation area. Black space, illuminated by billions of tiny pinpoints, completely engulfed him. Ignoring her wounds, Napoleon pulled her blue leotard off and went to him. They held each other a long time.

"Each of those dots is a star," Harlan said, seemingly ages later. "And around each of those stars are maybe a dozen planets. Somewhere, on one of them, is our home."

"Anywhere is our home," she told him. "With just one short stopover."

She looked up into his eyes, her whole existence reflected there. She smiled. "You can just call me the 'First in Line,'" she said.

EPILOGUE

Pound and Muse waited around until the child was born. Back on the first moon of Finally, Finally Over, Napoleon gave birth to a small, active, beautifully formed tiger-man, its fur fire yellow and its eyes powder blue.

"Feline genes are far more powerful than any in the universe," she told the happy father, his beard completely grown back, "Anyone knows that. Besides, it was you the Sorcerer Supreme changed, not me."

Pound and Muse stayed for the festivities and waited until the Federation ship came to show the new family the wonders of the inhabited universe. Then they trudged back to the refitted, redesigned starship. Mess' parting gift to the female computer was the ability and mechanisms to manifest herself. As it was, she floated beside her master in the form of a blinking ball.

Pound sat in the middle of his reconverted theater and sighed.

"What now?" Muse inquired.

" 'There are more things in heaven and earth,' " the director quoted, "than are dreamed of in your philosophy, my dear Muse. Let's say you and me take a little trip down a time stream or two. What do you say?"

"What do I say?" repeated the machine. "What do I say? I say, 'Aye! Verily!' "

"See to it, wench!" Pound cried, pulling himself up and shouting to the rafters. "Get this tub spaceworthy!"

Muse shot off in the direction of the control room to rev up the machinery. Pound watched her agile form disappear around a corner, then he sat down again. He leaned back in the plush red chair and cupped his chin in his hand. He thought for a moment, then smiled. Rising, he strode with energy onto his stage. Stopping in the middle, he whirled about and addressed his ship.

"All the universe is a stage,
And all the men, women, and aliens merely players.
They have their exits and their entrances;
But one man, in his time stream, can play many parts."

Roscoe Pound laughed.